The Tale of
the Magic Mole
and More

I0633685

Lee Pritchett

chipmunkapublishing
the mental health publisher

Published by
Chipmunkapublishing
United Kingdom

http://www.chipmunkapublishing.com

Copyright © 2014 Lee Pritchett

ISBN   978-1-78382-127-3

Chipmunkapublishing gratefully acknowledge the support of Arts Council England.

Contents

Stories

The Tale of The Magic Mole
Tobi, Mollie and The River Between Worlds
Mr Bumble and the Magic Pool
The Tale of Cerys Telling and The Yellow Bus.
Daniel's Day of Magic
Smitten The Kitten and The Fairy Fun Fair
Moona and The Talent Show
The Mystery of The Bonfire Ghost
The Land of Buttons and Milk
Holly and The Winter Match
Lucy and The Christmas Bear

Rhymes

The Adventure of Garry The Gobble
Spotty Backwing
Skybear and The Moon
The Epheline and The Fizzle Fairy
Princess Purdy's Birthday Cake
Eddie and The Biscuit Mines
Sydney The Super Hedgehog
Pudding Land
The Bear With the Magical Stone

Lee Pritchett

Prologue

My first published book was called 'The Tale of Greta Gumboot and Other Stories' and was a story collection very much like this one. The second book in this series was named 'Berty Tumblefluff and Friends'. There is also a third story collection by the name of 'Geoffrey Bumble and Friends'. This book, the fourth in the series is for children who have read the first three collections and new readers alike. Inside there is many a magical story and rhyme. Some of the stories continue from tales in the first three books, but some are brand new tales for you to enjoy. All the drawings are my own too. I hope you all enjoy reading it as much as I enjoyed writing it for you...

Lee Pritchett

Stories

Lee Pritchett

The Tale of The Magic Mole

As the good witch Greta Gumboot walked merrily through the forest, the plump little woman was suddenly overcome by a very funny feeling. Something was close, something magical. She couldn't see, hear or smell anything different, but she knew something was. All she could make out around her were the normal things she saw here every day. The path on which she stood was coated with a crisp carpet of brown and orange leaves, which crunched under the weight of her big brown magical boots. Around her were the tall bare trees of autumn and the still lush green rhododendron bushes of her magical wood. The last blue, yellow and white flowers of summer lingered at the side of the path. Suddenly she heard something. It was the distinct sound of another pair of feet crunching in her direction. Greta leaped behind the nearest rhododendron bush.

Once upon a time Greta had been a naughty witch and would've been hiding here to jump out on an unsuspecting creature, with a spell at hand to turn it into a chocolate bunny or perhaps a candy cane. These days Greta was a changed woman and all she was doing was hiding.

As the footsteps got ever closer, Greta took off her snow white pointed hat, revealing her shoulder length red hair. She was ready to conjure protection if needed. Greta's hat could produce all manner of things, from tennis balls to crystal balls, and also other things which weren't even round. Just being able to conjure round things would be a bit of a limiting factor for a witch, don't you think? Anyway, Greta crouched down low, afraid to peer out from behind the bush. She could still sense the same presence she had first felt and it was very close and seemed extremely powerful.

All of a sudden, the footsteps stopped and Greta heard a voice calling to her.

"Greta," it called "Hello. I know you're there. Hello."

"Who is it?" Greta cautiously replied.

"It is I," they replied "Strauss the mouse."

"Really?" said Greta, popping her head out from behind the bush. "Pheww...that explains it. I thought I sensed magic coming my way, but it's strange I didn't recognise it as you."

"Perhaps my powers have grown," he laughed "I am sure that is all, my friend."

"Indeed they seem to have." replied Greta, getting out from behind the bush and dusting off her long, purple dress "I sense a huge amount of magic around here. Wherever you're getting your power from, I'm glad you're on my side. How did you know I was here? Did you use magic?"

"Indeed not." He replied and pointed to the ground.

Greta saw the trail of scuffed leaves leading up to the bush and smiled.

"Silly me. I didn't think of that."

"Let us walk together now, Greta." he said and so they did.

The two friends walked all the way to Geoffrey Bumble's tree house. They found the old wizard using a shiny, steel shovel to clear up the many mounds of earth that had appeared scattered all around the base of the mighty oak tree, which held his rickety home. Geoffrey was dressed in purple trousers, his red cloak and orange boots. On top of his grey fluffy head of hair he wore his special purple hat with pink spots. Wilfred the little, grey furred wolf pup was running around, barking at each new pile that appeared

"What on earth happened here Geoffrey?" asked Greta.

"Indeed my friend." said Strauss. "You appear to have a problem."

Every time Geoffrey shovelled away a mound it would just pop back up with a fresh pile of dirt. He had obviously been at it for some time as the big pile, where he was shovelling the dirt onto, was nearly as tall as he was.

"They just don't want to go away." he complained, his face going pink with frustration. "Every time I clear one pile, another appears and more new piles are appearing all the time. I don't know what to do."

"Woof!" barked Wilfred.

"Calm down, Geoffrey." said Greta, placing a hand on his shoulder "You too, Wilfred. We'll get this sorted out somehow."

"It is only a little dirt, Geoff." said Strauss the Mouse.

"We'll just do a quick spell," smiled Greta "and we'll have this cleaned up in jiffy."

"I suppose I should have tried that," said Geoffrey, with a huff "but when I started there were only one or two of them so I thought I'd have a go at it the old fashioned way."

"Let me, my dear." said Greta. She raised her arms in the air and began to chant.

"The dirt all around, has begun to mount up.

It bothers our Geoffrey, and it bothers his pup.

Clean up all this mess, and set the ground free.

With a cool blowing breeze, one, two, three."

Instantly the wind began to blow fiercely.

"Bowwwwww...woof." Wilfred moaned and took cover behind Mr Bumble's oak tree.

Greta and Geoffrey held on to their hats as lots of tiny little whirlwinds appeared. One floated over each mound of earth. They sucked up all the loose earth and sparkled with brilliant, white energy as it evaporated into nothing. Then the whirlwinds disappeared as if they had never been there.

"Yay." shouted Mr Bumble, jumping about with joy. Then he quickly made himself calm down, looking very embarrassed.

"Sorry about that," he said, blushing "but sometimes you just can't contain yourself. I've had enough of cleaning up dirt for the time being. Wilfred's footprints in the house are bad enough, but...."

"Bow....woof...woof." yapped Wilfred running out from behind the tree and sitting at Geoffrey Bumble's feet. He made himself look as cute as possible.

"No, of course you're not a pain, Wilfred." said Geoffrey, feeling guilty "I didn't mean it like that."

Wilfred nuzzled at his ankles and gave a little "Woof."

"Oh, I love you too." said Geoffrey, kneeling down and tickling the little wolf pup behind the ears.

Suddenly the sound of popping echoed all around, causing everyone to jump. All the mounds of earth reappeared from the ground along with twice as many more. They were everywhere and they were spreading, more and more by the second. Trees and bushes began getting sucked down into the ground, all over the place. Even Mr Bumble's mighty oak began sinking.

"What on earth?" said Geoffrey "My house."

"Wooooof?" cried Wilfred, jumping again as a mound popped up, directly beneath him.

"Oh my," said Greta, sounding very worried "My spell seems to have aggravated things."

"Yes," said Strauss, "It appears we have a magical problem."

"Woof." said Wilfred.

"Yes my boy," replied Mr Bumble "The problem does appear to be growing."

"We must do something," said Greta, sounding panicked "quickly."

"But what?" asked Geoffrey.

"We could try another spell?" said Strauss.

"No," said Geoffrey "we need to know what we are up against first. We had better talk to Julius before this spell overtakes the whole wood."

They ran with all their might to Julius Beetroot's magical pool, finding the little squirrel paddling around the water with a huge leaf for a boat and sticks for oars.

"Hello, my friends." he said in his deep, hearty voice. "How may I help you all today?"

"Oh, Julius," said Greta "we have a terrible problem and it's heading this way."

"What, may I ask is this problem?" said the squirrel, jumping ashore. His little, blue cape flapped in the breeze as he did so.

"There's some kind of spell." Geoffrey told him.

"Yes." said Strauss. "Hundreds of dirt mounds are magically appearing in our wood, more by the moment. Trees and plants are being sucked down into the earth."

"They started at Geoffrey's tree house." said Greta. "I cast a spell to clean up the first few, but it backfired. Soon the whole wood will be dirt and all the trees and plants will be gone.

"This is indeed terrible." said Julius, calmly, "but I do not believe you are dealing with a spell."

"What do you mean?" asked Geoffrey.

"I believe it is a creature, you seek." he told them "A mole."

"A mole?" said Greta, sounding confused "How could one mole do so much damage?"

"It is not an ordinary mole." he told them.

"A magic mole?" said Strauss.

"Indeed." said Julius.

"Why is it doing this?" said Greta "How do we stop it?"

"These moles are very powerful creatures." he replied "The only way to stop him is to convince him to leave."

"Well," said Greta "How do we find him?"

"Call him with a spell." Julius replied. "Find out why he's doing this. Anyway, must be off."

"Julius," said Greta "Aren't you going to help us?"

"Not today, my dear." said Julius "I have great confidence in you...besides...I must start collecting some nuts for winter."

And with that he was off.

Greta gave a huge sigh and then said.

"How do we talk round such a powerful being? I mean, if he's set on destroying our wood, then why would he listen to us?"

"I think you can appeal to anyone's good nature." said Geoffrey, placing a reassuring hand on her shoulder."

"Indeed, my dear." added Strauss "You saved me from darkness, as you yourself were saved. You have a great gift."

"But the doves of peace saved you, really." said Greta "Wait a minute, we could use that spell on the mole."

"Afraid not, my dear." said Mr Bumble "From what Julius said, I don't think even that spell will work. Besides, it's locked up tightly in my tree house and I'm not sure if it's safe to go back. It's probably sunk all the way under by now, anyway. Blast it all."

"Ok," said Greta "let's try a calling spell, all together."

"I believe Julius Beetroot has entrusted this to you, Greta." said Strauss "I think you should call him by your own voice alone. But do not worry. We will be here if you need us."

"I agree," said Geoffrey, looking rather flustered "but I shall render assistance if needed."

"Ok," said Greta, raising her hands in the air "here goes."

"Mole of the earth, open your eyes.

Search your way through our wood, and hear my voice try,

To summon you here, to where I now stand,

Please pause from destroying, our lovely land.

For I ask that we talk. And discuss our wood.

Perhaps we could be friends, if we just understood."

For a moment nothing happened, but then they heard something. It was the popping sound of approaching mole hills. They were moving at super speed towards them and getting louder as they did so.

A trail of progressively bigger molehills shot up to the side of the stone around the pool. Then the three friends got a surprise. A tiny little mole, no bigger than a kitten came flying out of the final hill, jumping high in the air and landing on the stone beside them. He was cute, with white silky fur, which sparkled with glittery, white brilliance. Was this really a dark creature?"

"What do you want, lady?" he asked Greta, in his squeaky, little voice. "I got a lot of work to be on with."

"Wuff wuff wuff," said Wilfred "wooof wooof."

"No," said Geoffrey "it's not a baby rabbit, Wilfred. And I don't think he wants a pair of stilts, at present."

"You callin' me short, woofy boy?" said the mole, shaking a fist.

"Wuff." replied Wilfred, cowering back and covering his eyes.

"Ok," smiled the mole. "But don't say it again."

"My dear Mr Mole," said Greta "The reason we called is because of what you're doing to our wood."

"Your wood?" said the mole. "I'm not after any wood. It's just the dirt I want. Good quality stuff. Never seen better."

"Yes." said Greta, "But the wood is on the dirt, and you're destroying it all."

"Well, what do you expect." said the mole. "All them nasty trees are getting in my way."

"In the way?" spat Geoffrey, losing his cool. "My home's in one of those trees. Where are me and Wilfred going to live now?"

"Rowwwwwoooo?" Wilfred howled in agreement.

"Shut it, woofy boy?" said the mole. He waved a paw and suddenly Wilfred was even smaller than him."

"Row?" he yelped, pawing at Geoffrey's heels.

"How dare you?" said Geoffrey. "He's just a poor little pup. How can you do such a thing to an innocent creature?"

Then the mole laughed as with another wave of his paw, Geoffrey bumble found himself too no bigger than the mole.

"I say." he said striding up to the mole "how rude you are. Someone should teach you some manners. Throwing around magic like it's garden seed mix."

"And who's going to teach me?" asked the mole, poking him in the chest. "You?"

"I just might do that." said Geoffrey, poking him back.

"Now boys," said Greta "I'm sure we can sort this all out, nicely."

"How's that?" they said, together. They both looked rather annoyed.

"Woof." squeaked the little Wilfred.

"No, I don't like being small either, Wilfred." said Geoffrey, "but we'll have this all sorted out soon. Don't worry."

"Look," said the mole "I can't see we've got anythin' here to discuss, so I'm off." He turned to leave and Greta spoke.

"Wait," she said "perhaps if you told us why you want our forest, maybe we can find another way to help you."

"That's a pretty obvious one, really." said the mole. "I'm building a molehill?"

"A molehill?" Strauss asked him, "but you've already built hundreds. Why, my friend, do you need another one?"

"Hundreds?" said the Mole, looking confused. "Oh, you mean these?" he pointed to the little mounds of earth. "These are just the foundations. When I've finished there'll be one big one, a thousand times the size of all them put together."

"But why do you need such a big mole hill?" asked Greta.

"Gotta rebuild." The Mole told them, sadly. "My last mole palace got knocked down, by a giant seagull. The stupid blighter built a huge nest on top of it and it got squished. I was lucky to escape. So I've been looking for a new home for ages. Came across this place when I was just about ready to give up."

"You just want a home?" asked Greta, beginning to understand. "Then why don't you just live here with us, with the wood as it is? We'd be glad to have you here as a friend. Why do you need to destroy our homes?"

"Me, live in a wood?" laughed the mole. "Moles don't live in woods. Moles live in molehills. Magic moles live in mole palaces, under the earth."

"But my friend," said Strauss, "this place is as good as any palace, trust me."

"What do you mean?" asked the Mole, intrigued.

"Greta," said Strauss "tell him how I myself came to live here."

"Well," said Greta, scratching her chin "I think you're the one to tell that tale."
She smiled at him and he smiled back.

"I came here as a foreigner from a distant land. I too wanted to destroy the wood in a way. I was not too unlike yourself, but here I found peace and a home full of friends who care for me. My mind was changed by these wonderful people. If you wish a home, and it seems that you do, a home is not just a place, it is where you have people that care for you. If you destroy the whole wood then who here would come to care for you and what home would you have then?

The mole sat and thought.

"I don't know." he said "I had had my mind set on a new palace."

"What better palace is there than a home full of people that love you?" said Greta.

"Love me?" said the mole, looking surprised "I could have a home full of friends who love me, like a family?"

"Indeed." smiled Strauss.

"Ok then." said the mole, glowing brighter than ever.

"Hello." said Geoffrey. "What about me?

"Woof?" added Wilfred.

"Of course I mean you too." said Geoffrey. The mole waved his paw and they were full sized again.

Greta picked up the little mole and gave him a huge hug,

"Thank you, my dear." Greta said, joyfully.

"Call me Monty." smiled the mole.

And with that all of the molehills disappeared. They all headed back to Greta Gumboot's cottage for cake and hot chocolate to welcome their new friend.

On the way they passed Mr Bumble's tree house, finding it as good as new. Not only were the molehills gone, but all of the trees, plants and flowers were back in their rightful place. The wood looked even more beautiful than it had earlier that day. And what a wonderful day it had turned out to be...

The End

Lee Pritchett

Tobi, Mollie and The River Between Worlds

It was Saturday evening and little Tobi had been playing games all day with his big sister. They'd play at pirates, spacemen and cowboys but Tobi's favourite game was a new one they'd made up that very day. They called it river worlding. Taking turns they had to get inside the cardboard box boat and paddle down the world river to a new land full of fun. That world gave them a whole new game to play, climbing mountains, swimming in the seas and even tunnelling deep beneath the earth in underground worlds. Tobi had eaten his dinner some time ago and now it was bedtime. His mummy gave him and his sister a glass of milk and a biscuit each, then they brushed their teeth, ready for bed.

As soon as Tobi's head hit the pillow he found himself drifting gently to sleep. A few moments later Tobi awoke to the splashing and lapping of water.

"Wake up, Tobi." said Mollie "Wake up. We're here."

Tobi opened his eyes, sleepily and said "Here? Here where?"

"On the river," she told him.

Toby Jumped up frantically, fully awake now. "What's going on?" he said "We're boating and I'm still in my stripy pyjamas."

"I know, silly." said Mollie, making her hair into pig tails. She was dressed in white pyjamas with pink polka dots. "At least I brought my scrunchies."

"I didn't bring anything." said Tobi, looking sad, "not even my....wait a minute.." he walked down to the end of the long, slender, golden boat and picked something up. "I did bring it." he said, with a grin "Trunky, my elephant."

He hugged the toy tightly. "I'm so glad you're here." he said.

"I'm glad you're here too." said Mollie.

"I was talking to Trunky." said Tobi "But I'm very glad you're here too, big sis. I wonder why mummy didn't pack us a lunch. She always does that when we go on a trip."

"I don't think she knew we were coming here." said Mollie. "It's not every night you go travelling on the World River."

"So this is the World River?" said Tobi.

"Of course it is." said Mollie "Where did you think we were?"

"I just told you." said Tobi, looking confused.

Mollie laughed. "Ok, so I guess we should make the most of it. Shall we go ashore?

Tobi looked over at the passing banks on either side. The scenery was changing so quickly. One minute there were trees and mountains, the next there were tall skyscrapers of a thousand brilliant colours. Strange animals roamed the riverbanks, like purple elephants and a creature that looked half dog and half kangaroo. This creature waved at them and the children waved back.

"What a lovely...eh...dogaroo." said Mollie. "Shall we go over and see him."

Tobi covered his mouth and whispered quietly. "I don't trust him. Looks like a sweetie stealer."

"But we don't have any sweeties." said Mollie.

"But we might get some." said Tobi "You never know."

"Ok." said Mollie, scratching her head "then you pick somewhere."

"How about there?" said Tobi, pointing to a beach where three orange seals were playing."

"Ok," said Mollie "grab an oar."

They both did so and they paddled their way over to the beach. The seals clapped as they came over and pulled the boat up on the sand.

"My greetings." said the smallest seal.

"Hello," said the children "It's nice to meet you."

"The pleasure is all ours," said another, much larger seal, wearing a bowler hat. We are grateful to receive a visit from such polite earthlanders. But still, you're going to have to go and check in at reception."

"Reception?" asked Tobi. "Aren't you the reception? You are right on the world river."

"Oh, no," said the small seal, we just like the water. Most new arrivals to our land come by toboggan."

"Toboggan?" asked Mollie. "Tobogganing between worlds?"

"Yes," said the larger seal. "but the mountain is extremely steep. I think you made the right choice, coming by river."

"The reception is a few miles that way." said the seal pointing inland. "We'll look after your boat for you."

"Thank you very much." said Mollie.

"You won't scratch it, will you?" said Tobi "We only just got it."

The seal laughed at this.

"Come on, Tobi." said Mollie and with that they headed off for the reception desk.

They hadn't been walking for long when they came to a huge pile of tiny pebbles. It was kind of hollow in the middle and was lined with sticks. It was almost like a giant nest.

The children climbed inside and took a look around.

"Do you think a giant bird lives here?" asked Tobi.

"Maybe." said Mollie "I think we had better get going, quickly."

"Oh, alright." said Tobi, reluctantly "But this place is really interesting."

As they went to climb out the other side, something caught Tobi's eye.

Something was glimmering at him from in amongst the sticks. He reached in and pulled it out.

"Wow." he said "It's a little chocolate egg." It was shiny and silver and warm to the touch.

"Lucky you." said Mollie, with a smile "I wish *I'd* found a chocolate egg."

"I'll share it with you later." said Tobi "Let's take a look round, first. We can have it after we check in."

"Ok." said Mollie. And they continued with their travels.

A little while later they came across a giant, rectangular, blue trampoline. It was the size of a football field and sunken into the ground."

"How do we get across this?" Tobi asked his sister.

"I guess we bounce." said Mollie. And with that she was off, springing across the trampoline.

Tobi followed her and they bounced higher and higher as they went.

"Weeeeeeeeeeeeeeee." shouted Tobi. "This is great."

"Weeeeeeeeee." said Mollie, equally enjoying herself. "I can see for miles from up here."

"I can see the toboggan mountain." said Tobi "Weeeeeeeeeeee."

"I can see lots of forest." said Mollie "Weeeeeeeeeeee."

"I can see...can see." Tobi began, going pale.

"See what?" asked Mollie "Weeeeeeeeee."

"A g-g-g giant."

"What?" asked Mollie, looking round to see for herself.

"He looks very angry and he's coming this way."

"Quick," said Mollie "run back to the boat."

"We can't," said Tobi, panicking "he's blocking our path. Head for the mountain."

"What?" said Mollie.

"If you can get in that way," said Tobi "then maybe you can get out."

"Good idea." said Mollie and off they bounced.

"Come back." shouted the giant, angrily "I'll teach you to bounce on my trampoline, Hooligans."

Mollie and Tobi were quickly off the trampoline, running for their lives.

Soon they found themselves running in a sort of mini desert where a giant baby was playing with a large tree as a rattle.

"Get outa my son's sand box." shouted the giant, bearded man. He was getting closer now.

"Goo goo goo." Went the baby and then he pointed at the children and burst out laughing.

"Keep running." said Mollie.

And soon they were sprinting through a dense forest, full of creeping vines and tiny, blue monkeys, swinging in the trees.

The monkeys laughed at them too, but soon stopped laughing went they saw the huge giant, thundering their way.

"Oh bother." screamed one of them and the monkeys fled off in all directions.

The giant was now quickly gaining on the children. Another minute and he'd have them in his grasp. Then all of a sudden the giant's thunderous footsteps stopped. The baby giant had started crying, loudly.

"It's ok, son." said the giant man, "daddy's coming. I'll catch up with you in just a second." he shouted to Tobi and Mollie.

As the giant turned round and went to his son, the two children stopped to catch their breath.

"That was lucky," said Mollie "he almost caught us."

"What do we do now, Mollie?" asked Tobi.

She took one more deep breath and said "Keep running."

And with that, they did.

Soon they were out of the forest and on open, grassy ground, nearing the base of the mountain.

"Can you see anything that looks like a reception?" Mollie asked her brother.

"Don't ask me," he said "I'm only five. How am I supposed to know what a reception looks like, particularly in a land with giants and talking seals?"

"Don't be so silly, Tobi." said Mollie "Anyone can spot a reception. It looks like...like."

"You can't spot it either." he said as they ran. "Wait a minute...Is that what a reception looks like?" he pointed ahead of them."

"Where?" asked Mollie.

"That thing." said Tobi.

"Oh," said Mollie, "You're right." A little, round hut had suddenly come into view at the base of the mountain. The occasional little toboggan could be seen, appearing in a flash at the snowy mountain top and zooming down to earth. "This is great." she said "We'll be there in a couple of minutes and the giant is nowhere to be seen."

Just then, there was a thundering in the distance. The giant was back on their trail, and from the sound of it, the rest had done him good. His footsteps were thundering faster than ever. The children looked over their shoulders and could see him, about to come out of the forest.

"Faster." shouted Mollie, "Run as fast as you can."

"That's easy for you to say." said Tobi, struggling to keep up "You're three years older than me, your legs are longer than mine and you do running at school."

"Stop complaining..." panted Mollie "and keep running."

They arrived at the little, blue hut in record time. They were met by a very large, brown, feathery duck, with round glasses on, peering at them over the counter.

"Slow down, you too." said the duck, sounding like it had a sore throat. "What can I do for you?"

"We need to get out of here." said Tobi.

"There's a giant after us." said Mollie.

"Oh, not him again." said the duck "he scares away all the tourists." Then the duck gave a huff "how will you be paying?"

"Paying?" asked the children, looking worried.

"Yes." said the duck "we take gold coins or egg stars."

"Come here." shouted the giant, he would be there in about twenty seconds.

"We don't have either of those things." said Mollie, "How about a scrunchy?" she said, pulling one out of her hair.

"Do my feathers really look that bad?" complained the duck.

Tobi thought for a moment and said "How about this?" he reached into his pocket and pulled out the chocolate egg he had found earlier. He handed it to the duck.

"Well, well," said the duck "I haven't seen a platinum egg star in years. The duck cracked the egg on the counter and a brilliant little silver star flew out of the egg, floating in the air.

A silver toboggan, big enough for two appeared beside the children.

"Get on." said the duck and they quickly did so.

Just as the giant had them in reach and was about to grab them, the toboggan zoomed off up the mountain at light speed, disappearing at the top.

Tobi woke up with a start. It was morning now and he jumped out of bed to find his sister.

They ran right into each other in the hallway and fell over. She had also been looking for him.

"Did we just..?" Tobi began.

"I think we did, you know." replied Mollie "I think we did..."

The End

Lee Pritchett

Mr Bumble and The Magic Pool

It was a hot summer's day in the magical woodland and the rhododendrons were blooming all over with brilliant blue pink and white flowers. Mr Bumble was out tending to his flower bed at the base of the mighty oak tree that held his rickety tree house. He was dressed in purple trousers and a purple, spotty t-shirt, which matched his purple, pointed wizard's hat with its accidentally created, pink spots. Geoffrey had got used to the spots and quite liked them these days. The yellow pansies in the bed were humming, softly to themselves, like flowers do. Wilfred the fluffy grey little wolf pup was running about the grassy ground, chasing the butterflies.

"What a lovely day it is." Mr Bumble said to the little pup.

"Woof wooo rooooo." Wilfred barked, stopping his chasing activities.

"Yes I agree." said Geoffrey, wiping his forehead "perhaps it is just a little too hot."

"Woof woooo." said Wilfred.

"Swimming?" asked Mr Bumble "Where could we go swimming? There's only that very large pool of my old washing up water on the other side of the wood, hmm... I really must do something about that."

"Wooof." barked Wilfred.

"There's somewhere else?" repeated Mr Bumble "Where?"

"Woof woof wurrrr." said Wilfred, cheekily.

"Julius's pool?" said Geoffrey, sounding concerned "We can't go there. I don't think the little squirrel would be very happy about it. And besides that, it's magic. Anything could happen."

"Woof woof." said Wilfred.

"How do you know nothing will happen?" said Geoffrey.

"Woof," said Wilfred "woof, woof."

"I know Greta went in there and came out fine," Geoffrey replied "but look what happened to her. She took a trip to another world."

"Woof." said Wilfred, wagging his tail.

"Why are you sure it won't happen to us?" asked Geoffrey looking confused. "I'm the wizard here, you know."

"Wurrrruffff." woofed Wilfred.

"Well." said Geoffrey, scratching his chin. "I suppose that does make a difference. Greta did take that journey because she needed to learn a lesson. We don't need to learn a lesson, do we?"

"Woof." said Wilfred, bouncing about with excitement.

"Ok," said Geoffrey "I'll just pop upstairs and get a pair of shorts. Then we can go and ask Julius if we can take a dip in his pool. But if he says no that's it, no arguments from you."

Wilfred just wagged his tail and stared at Geoffrey as if to say "Hurry up."

"I don't know what's gotten in to him, lately." said Geoffrey, as he climbed the wooden ladder up to his tree house.

A few minutes later he came back down, still dressed in his purple, spotty hat, but now wearing only a matching pair of shorts and sandals with it. On his face he wore a pair of round framed sunglasses and carried a purple beach towel over one arm.

Wilfred barked and ran off ahead of him, headed for Julius Beetroot's pool.

"Wait for me." called Geoffrey, running after him.

About half way to Julius's magic pool, Geoffrey found something on the ground. It was a shiny copper penny.

"How strange to see money inside our wood." he said, picking up the coin "I wonder who dropped it."

"Woof." replied Wilfred.

"Yes." said Geoffrey flicking the coin in the air and catching it again "I believe it is good luck."

They carried on walking and a few minutes later they came across a stranger in the wood. It was a little old man. He was hunched over and using a walking-stick. The man was dressed in long, dark red robes, with a golden sun on the chest.

"Good day, my friend." said the fellow, in a deep rasping voice. It was just then that Mr Bumble noticed that the man was in need of a shave and his eyes shone green. This was possibly a sign of dark magic, but maybe not."

"Woof." said Wilfred.

"Sorry," said the man, "didn't mean to ignore you, little fellow."

The exact way he responded made it sound like he understood what the pup had said. 'Hmmm." thought Geoffrey.

"You haven't seen an old penny lying around here anywhere, have you?" asked the man "It has deep, sentimental value to me, you see."

Geoffrey had the strongest feeling that he should just hand it over, but decided that he didn't trust the man. Besides, he liked his new lucky penny.

"No," he said, "sorry. We'll just be on our way."

"Ok," said the man, "thank you very much for your time. You will let me know if you see it? I'll be...around."

Geoffrey didn't like the way the man said 'around' and he hurriedly led Wilfred off, heading on towards Julius's magic pool."

Ten minutes later they arrived at the little pool, in a quiet clearing, sunken deep into a huge flat, sandy coloured rock in the ground. There was no sign of Julius Beetroot anywhere.

"Hello, Julius," called Geoffrey "are you there?"

"Rowwoooo." called Wilfred, but there was no reply.

"Looks like he's not here." said Geoffrey, turning to leave "Come on, we'll come back another time."

"Ro?" said Wilfred.

"What do you mean why?" said Geoffrey. "I told you we can't go in there without Julius's say so."

"Rowooo." moaned Wilfred.

"A little dip?" asked Geoffrey, looking thoughtful. "Well maybe it couldn't hurt."

Wilfred just stared at him, lovingly.

"Oh, ok." said Geoffrey, "but just a few minutes to cool off, then we're out and gone."

"Woof," Wilfred agreed and he jumped straight into the water, with a plop.

Geoffrey took off his sandals and sun glasses and carefully dipped a toe in, to see what the water was like.

"Just right." he said and lowered himself in to the water, forgetting to take the lucky penny out of his pocket. Geoffrey and Wilfred were enjoying their morning swim in the cool water when something terrible happened.

The water began to swirl into a great whirlpool, sucking the two friends down into the depths, just like it had done to Greta all that time ago. There was no fighting its mighty pull. Unlike when Greta entered the pool, Geoffrey and Wilfred completely disappeared when they reached the bottom. Julius just tutted to himself, from a high branch, overhead.

Geoffrey and Wilfred found themselves waking up in the depths of a strange underwater kingdom. It was an ocean of pure, clear blue water, where the sea bed was covered with millions of lucky pennies of all different sizes. Some were regular sized, but others were big enough to be a chariot wheel or a pizza.

By magic the two of them had no trouble breathing and felt totally fine.

"I wonder where we are?" said Geoffrey.

"Woof." replied Wilfred, swimming down to the ocean bed.

"Pennyland?" asked Geoffrey "Well, I suppose that is quite a good name. What are you doing?"

Wilfred had hold of a huge penny and was carrying it up to his master.

"Well, thank you." said Geoffrey, taking it from him "but I'm not sure if I can keep it, really."

"You there." shouted a voice from the distance. Geoffrey turned to see a large group of trident armed mermen headed their way. "Stop, thief." they yelled. "Stealer of the queen's lucky pennies."

"Oh no." said Geoffrey "Better get out of here. Let me try a spell.

We're under the sea. We need to get out.
But up is no good. It's just messing about.
We need to fly far, back to our wood
Away from these mermen. Here our chances aren't good.
Transport us by magic, like the way we came here.
With a flash of bright light, make us disappear."

There was certainly a bright flash of white light, and a lot of bubbles but that was it.

"What's going on?" Geoffrey said, frantically.

"Ro ro rowww." replied Wilfred, his tail between his legs.

"You can have it back." called Geoffrey, holding the giant coin out to them "We didn't mean any harm."

Mr Bumble jumped to one side as one of the mermen threw a heavy, iron trident his way, just missing him and Wilfred.

"Run, boy." he cried out loud and they took off in the opposite direction to the mermen.

"Row roo roo?" said Wilfred, as they fled.

"Ok," panted Geoffrey "I mean swim. Happy now?"

"Woof." replied the little wolf pup.

Geoffrey and Wilfred swam with all their might, past giant, golden statues of mermen and through a shoal of a thousand brilliant, shimmering golden fish.

"Excuse me," said Geoffrey, to the fish "we're in a spot of bother. Is there any chance you could lend a hand."

The fish seemed all too happy to swan about, acting pretty, but remarkably unwilling to do anything to help. Geoffrey felt quite sure he heard one of them laugh at him, so on they swam. They swam and they swam, for what seemed like miles, past more coins and more statues and more unhelpful fish that obviously had ambitions toward getting modelling contracts.

All the time they could hear the mermen splashing and shouting, not far behind them.

The wizard and his pup were getting more tired with every minute and the mermen were now closing the gap.

"Stop." they called "In the name of lady luck, we command the thieves to stop and accept their punishment, like the fiends they are."

With that three more tridents came flying their way.

Geoffrey and Wilfred only just managed to avoid them. They were even closer then the last one.

"Good shot, Brian." They heard one merman tell another.

"Why thank you, Sid." said another one, with a very posh accent "Marvellous, wasn't it?"

"Look Wilfred." said Geoffrey, still holding his new, supposedly lucky penny.

There was a huge statue up ahead. It was ten times bigger than the others. The huge amount of giant, house sized pennies piled up, wonkily around its base, made it look more like a mountain. It was like a beacon of hope to Geoffrey.

"If we can get behind that," he said "then maybe we can lose the mermen and find somewhere to hide and sort this all out."

"Woof." barked Wilfred.

"Yes," agreed Geoffrey "It is a good idea, isn't it."

The two friends made one last push, swimming with all their might and just managing to stay ahead of the mermen. As they reached the mountain statue, the creatures were only about thirty seconds behind them.

"Come back." the mermen shouted, one last time, as Geoffrey and Wilfred ducked round behind the statue. A few more tridents clattered against the giant pennies.

Geoffrey quickly began searching around the nooks and crannies between the coins and soon found somewhere he deemed to be the perfect hiding place. Down in a crevasse between some of the huge, metal disks he found a dark cave.

"Come on down, boy." he called to Wilfred, who was searching elsewhere. "I've found the perfect place."

"Woof." said Wilfred, Swimming down after him, and in they went.

"Complete quiet now, Wilfred." said Mr Bumble "Not a sound."

"Wuff." agreed Wilfred, as quietly as possible.

A few seconds later they heard splashing up above.

"Where'd they go, captain?" one merman said to another.

"This I am not sure of," he replied "but we shall find them. Take half the patrol. Search the area, thoroughly. I will report back to the queen. Thieves shall not be tolerated here."

They heard more splashing as the men moved off to begin their search.

"Woof woof." said Wilfred.

"Yes," said Geoffrey "we can't stay here long. We need a way to escape without them seeing us. I suppose I could try a spell, but after that last one I..."

Suddenly there was a huge bang as the entrance to the cave slammed shut and the huge, copper whale heaved itself up from under the weight of the huge pennies.

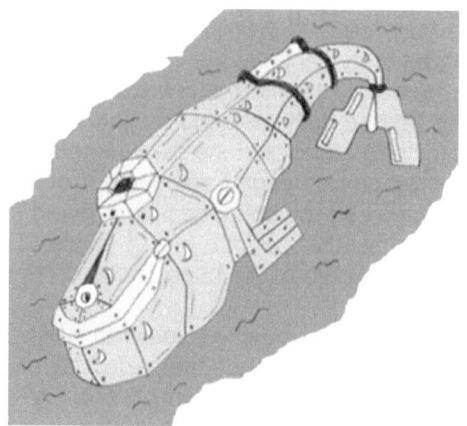

"Ah," said Geoffrey, standing in complete darkness."I believe I may have made a miscalculation."

"Wooof." agreed Wilfred.

But then suddenly all of the water drained out of the room and they found themselves perfectly dry.

"Well," said Geoffrey "That's better. I'll just see if I can find a light switch."

He fumbled about a bit in the dark and said "Here it is."

He pulled on the chord and a light did indeed come on. The two friends found themselves in a small, oval shaped room, with shining, copper walls and a padded, leather bench running around the outside. There was a table at the far end of the room with a pot of tea for Geoffrey, and a plate of biscuits. A bowl of fresh water was under the table for Wilfred.

"I say," said Geoffrey "this is very civilized. "

He sat down and poured himself a cup. Wilfred had a drink too.

"Welcome to copper whale, flight one-o- three." said a voice over the loud speaker. "Tea and biscuit facilities are free but there is a small charge for complimentary key-chains. Two small key-rings appeared on the table with little copper pennies on their chains."

"Well thank you, dear fellow." said Geoffrey "But I haven't figured out what to do with this big coin yet. The mermen are mad at me for taking it, but they won't let me give it back."

"I'm very sorry to hear that, sir." said the Whale "Perhaps a trip to the palace is in order."

"You mean you're going to turn us in?" said Mr Bumble, with fright.

"Rooooooooo." cried Wilfred.

"My goodness, no." replied the whale, "Very rude, mermaids, the lot of them. What I mean is if you sneak into the palace, you'll be ok. I can drop you right outside."

"Why would we want to sneak inside the palace?" asked Geoffrey.

"To give the coin back." said the whale "It's the only way they'll take it. If you put it in the queen's money box she'll even grant you a wish. I believe you wanted to go somewhere?"

"Fantastic." smiled Geoffrey "Best news I've heard all day. All we have to do is sneak past an armed guard into the palace and... hmmm... This doesn't sound so easy."

"You'll be fine." said the whale.

"Woof." added Wilfred, wagging his tail.

"I'm glad you're confident, anyway." said Geoffrey, sounding glum.

The whale swam on for about an hour then opened his mouth and said "Here we are. Out you get then."

For some reason the water wasn't coming inside.

"Will we still be able to breathe out there?" asked Geoffrey.

"Of course." said the whale, sounding surprised. "Everyone can breathe underwater in this world."

"Woof." said Wilfred, munching down one last biscuit.

"Thank you very much, dear whale." said Geoffrey "You've been most kind."

"Aw." said the whale "I'll tell you what, the key-chains are on me."

Geoffrey put them in his pocket and said "You're a true gentleman." They got out and waved goodbye. The two friends now found themselves at the huge, iron gates of a

41

gigantic spiral shell shaped palace. It was made out of shining copper and mother of pearl.

"Now remember," said Geoffrey "quiet." and with that they swam up and over the palace wall. They couldn't see any guards in the courtyard so headed for the main door. Just as they got close, two armed guards swam out and took up position in front of the door. Luckily Geoffrey and Wilfred hadn't been spotted. The door shut tightly behind the guards, making a loud locking sound.

"We'll have to go in through a window." said Geoffrey, "But we need a distraction. I know..."

He took a key-ring and threw it to the far side of the yard. It landed with a resonating ping that sent a huge shockwave of white energy rippling though the courtyard. Geoffrey hadn't known the key-rings were magic.

"Woof." said Wilfred, pointing to the guards.

"You're right," said Geoffrey "they are asleep. Let's get going before they wake up. I really must send that whale a thank you card."

The two friends swam upwards, looking for the window of an empty room. It didn't seem like there were too many people around, inside the palace. And carefully staying out of sight of the mermaids they did see, they soon found a clear way to enter.

"This will do nicely." said Geoffrey, pointing to the little window.

"Wooof." Wilfred told him.

"Yes," said Geoffrey "I'll go inside first. Scaredy-cat." he said with a little chuckle.

"Wuff?" asked Wilfred.

"Oh, nothing." said Geoffrey, swimming carefully through the window. Wilfred waited outside for a moment.

"It's alright," said Geoffrey "the coast is clear."

The pup swam in cautiously, finding that he and Geoffrey were on the palace's, third floor landing. The inside of the castle was made out of the purest, solid, white marble. The walls were hung with engraved plates of copper. The landing was like a huge shelf, running round the outside of the room and they could see straight down into the main entrance hall. There was an incredibly steep, marble staircase going down into the huge chamber and at the bottom of the stairs they saw just what they were looking for.

"It's the money box." said Geoffrey. "We've found it, Wilfred. Surprising though, it doesn't look very well protected."

"Woof." said Wilfred, quietly.

"Yes." replied Geoffrey. He patted the huge, copper penny he was still carrying "I agree. Let's get this over with."

They quietly made their way down the stairs approaching the huge golden treasure chest, wrapped in silver chains.

"Here goes nothing." said Geoffrey, when they reached the bottom. He raised the coin towards the huge slot in the top of the chest.

Just as the coin was about to enter the slot, there was a bright flash and Geoffrey was thrown backward, dropping the penny.

Then alarm bells started to ring all around.

"Ro ro." woofed Wilfred.

Geoffrey had to think fast. He took the last key-chain from his pocket and threw it at the moneybox. The whole thing shimmered with white light. Hopefully it would accept the coin now."

Geoffrey quickly picked up the coin, but before he could put it in the slot, merman and mermaid guards rushed in all around them.

"Not so fast, you terrible foes of the crown." said the captain. He now carried a golden trident "We've got you now."

"But we really didn't mean any harm." said Geoffrey, sounding scared.

Wilfred remained silent, behind Geoffrey's back. "Please," he said "take the coin and let us go."

"You're not going anywhere." said one of the mermaids, holding a golden spear. "You're our prisoners now."

'There's no way I can get the coin in that slot,' thought Mr Bumble 'not without being hit by a spear, but maybe...just maybe.'

As the mermaids moved in closer, Geoffrey carefully slipped the coin behind his back and began to gently offer it to Wilfred. For a moment the pup didn't get it, but suddenly he realised. The petite little fellow grabbed the coin, jumping up on top of the moneybox at lightning speed.

"Nooooo!" cried the mermen, as he dropped it in the slot, but then it was too late.

"The palace was suddenly filled with a warm, orange glow as a chubby little mer-woman, in a brilliant copper and emerald crown made her way down the stairs. In one hand she held an ornate, copper sceptre, with a large ruby on top.

All of the mer-people bowed to her and Geoffrey thought he had better do the same.

"What are your names?" asked the queen.

"I'm Geoffrey, your majesty," said Mr Bumble "and this is Wilfred. We are most honoured to meet you."

"Hmm," said the queen, in a very posh accent "Geoffrey and Wilfred, you may have stolen from us, but you have also proven yourselves to be worthy creatures. I shall grant you but one wish. So use it carefully."

"You are most gracious, my lady." said Geoffrey, getting up. "I am very sorry for taking one of your lucky pennies and I assure you that it will never happen again."

"As well it should not." said the queen. "What would you ask of me?"

"Roooo." woofed Wilfred.

"You want to go home?" asked the queen. "Is that all? Wouldn't you prefer rubies or emeralds?"

"I think we've had quite enough of treasure for one day." said Geoffrey "Home would be fine."

"Indeed." said the queen, with a smile.

She raised her sceptre high above her head and called out loud.

"Away you go, travellers of land.
Back from where you came.
The water is the place for us,
But for you it's not the same."

There was a bright flash of pink light and the two friends magically disappeared.

Geoffrey and Wilfred each took a huge breath as they splashed up through the surface of the woodland pool.

Julius was standing on the bank, watching them.

"My dear friends." he said "Have you had a nice swim?"

"Oh, Julius." said Geoffrey "You wouldn't believe it if I told you."

"I think I would." said Julius, transforming into the red robed old man they'd met earlier.

"Oh, my goodness," said Geoffrey, jumping back. "It was you, I... I... have something of yours, don't I?"

He took the man's penny from his pocket and quickly gave it back to him.

"I'm so sorry," said Geoffrey "deeply, deeply sorry for taking it and for swimming in your pool without asking."

"Well," replied Julius, transforming back into himself again "It would seem that your trip wasn't wasted."

"You know about our trip?" said Geoffrey, getting out of the water and lifting Wilfred out after him. The pup shook himself dry and started chasing butterflies again.

The squirrel just looked at him, knowingly.

"Julius," asked Geoffrey "that wasn't a wishing penny, was it?"

"That would be telling, my good fellow." said Julius "That would be telling..."

The End

The Tale of Cerys Telling and The Yellow Bus

Part 1: A Case of Pencils

"Hello everyone. My name's Cerys Telling. It's been a while since we first talked. I'm a very special little hamster girl. Well, actually I'm a big girl now. I just turned four.

Since my birthday things have become odd at home. Mummy has been collecting up pens and pencils and putting them in a little, fluffy case. She says that it is for me. I think that the pink is very pretty, but that is not the point. What is it for? "

Part 2: A few days later

"Mummy put the fluffy case inside a pretty backpack in the shape of a pony. My lunch is in there too, along with my bunny shaped drawing pad. How I do like a good fluffy bunny.

Back to the point. I do like ponies but I also like my lunch out where I can eat it. I'm sure that the pony isn't hungry now but how does this help me? Is this feeding of the pony to happen every day, like bath time?

Oh no. Now Kato cat is feeding the pony my sweeties. Kato, no, that's a bad kitty. Oh, I'll have to get them back out later.

Mummy, Daddy, What do you mean *I'm* going on a bus? Aren't you coming with me? I'm only little, you know. Someone might steal my pony.

The bus is going to be full of children? Nooooooo. And it's yellow? I like yellow. Stop taunting me with yellow. Don't make me go. You can't make me go."

Part 3: On the bus

"Ok, they made me go. I may have a pony but I'm not going to enjoy it.

Oh my. These children are talking to me. They're singing and playing. I'm having fun if I ignore the smelly bus driver. *Pew*, old socks.

This is great. I feel like dancing, running and having fun. I love my new friends.

What was that?
Oh. Ok Mrs Bus driver lady, I'll stop running now. Spoil sport."

Part 4: At School

"Oh my, even more children and interesting grownups too. They know smart stuff like how to stick glitter to your face. But what is this? More running? More playing? Boys eating worms? Hmmm I sense an opportunity here.
No, brainy Billy you can't have any sweets. Unless...
Oh alright, I'll share, but you have to help me with my homework.
For how long?
A week... maybe two.
What? I must start my schooling off right. Kato would be proud. I'm sure of it. All behold the mighty power of the pony. Neigh........"

The End

Lee Pritchett

Daniel's day of magic

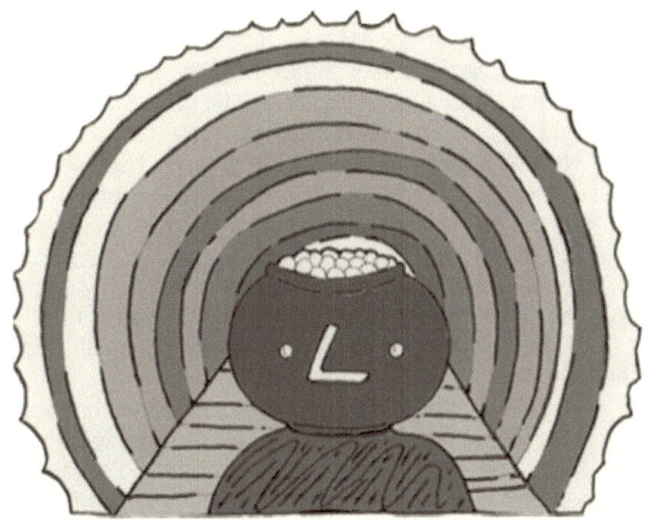

Today was a warm summer's day in the village of Sky's End. Eight-year-old Daniel Winston decided to go for a walk in the forest just outside of town. He was dressed in a short sleeved red t-shirt, blue shorts and his favourite white trainers. Sky's End was a rather unusually named village but everyone was friendly if a little quirky. Daniel's own mother, Doris Winston, spent her life baking sparkling pink cakes. They were always big enough to contain a sizable baby elephant. They never had any houseguests but Daniel and his father rarely got a piece of cake anyway. They always got eaten by somebody, or maybe something. You couldn't tell really. It was always right when nobody was paying any particular attention. All of a sudden, poof they were gone.

As Daniel walked through the forest the noisy and particularly shiny bumble bees set him on edge a little. They were buzzing from golden flower to golden flower. Still, young Daniel was enjoying the sunshine. The cool breeze was nice too. He thought the forest was really beautiful. The smell of the rich greenery was lovely. The sheer amount of clover on the ground made Daniel feel very lucky indeed.

Daniel walked deeper and deeper into the forest. He listened to the strangely well hidden birds whistle and clang. Yes, the clanging was rather odd. He and all the other town folk were pretty used to it, so Daniel gave the matter no real thought.

He was walking by a very tall group of trees with rich red bark when something began to creak. The boy jumped with fright as one of the tremendous trunked trees came crashing to the ground. It landed next to him with a gigantic bang. Daniel dived to earth to escape the mighty impact. Believe me, it was pretty close, but luckily he wasn't hurt.

"Phew," said Daniel. "Thank heavens for the lucky clover. I wonder how that happened."

Then something even more unexpected happened to him. A very high pitched, little Irish voice called to him.
"Sorry about that, little laddy. I told Shamus the whole tree t'ing was a daft idea but he wouldn't listen to an old fella like me."

"That's strange." Daniel said to the old man, "Why are you so short?"

"Short is it now?" said the little old man, who was now standing beside Daniel. The tiny fellow was dressed all in green, with a gold belt and matching shoe buckles. "You hurt me feelings a mite." he said, stroking his long, grey beard "You'd do well not pick on a leprechaun like that. You won't get any gold that way."

"A leprechaun." gasped Daniel, "You've got a pot of gold?" then he paused for a second "Wait a minute. Is there more of you? Do you like cake by any chance?"

"Me name's O'Leary, lad "said the leprechaun, clearly avoiding the question, "and I think I can go one better than a lone pot. This is Sky's End, you know."

"What do you mean?" asked the excited Daniel.

"You mean, you don't know? Did yer mammy never tell you tales at bedtime?"

"Not really" replied Daniel, sounding a little bit annoyed. "I always wanted her to but she's always been too busy baking."

"Well..." said the leprechaun, "Let's um...leave that matter for the moment, shall we?" Would you like to see the factory?"

"What factory?" asked Daniel.

"Come with me." said O'Leary and he led him up onto the stump of the fallen tree. "It's been sliced clean off." said Daniel, with surprise.

"In a way." replied O'Leary, "You'll soon see."

Daniel knelt down to feel the stump. It actually felt more like coloured plastic than wood.

Now they were both on the plastic platform, O'Leary banged his foot. 'This stump is definitely hollow' thought Daniel, 'judging by that sound.'

"SHAMUS. TWO COMING DOWN." O'Leary called.

Daniel was shocked as the trunk began sinking down into the ground like an elevator.

It was an elevator in fact. Daniel found himself descending down into a massive, round underground workshop. It must have run under the entire forest. Hundreds of conveyer belts swirled around the outside. They were loaded with thousands of glittering, sparkling, gold filled pots. There was an island in the middle covered in piles of stacked up pots of gold. In the centre of the island was a little, silver and glass building. It looked like a miniature office block, about twelve feet tall. All around the giant workshop there were thousands of identically dressed leprechauns. They were tending to the enormous pots of glimmering golden coins.

When they arrived at the island in the centre, Shamus apologised to Daniel for O'Leary nearly squishing him.

"You need to be more careful when you go out for a breather." he said, waving a finger at his co-worker.

It turned out that the two leprechauns were brothers. Shamus was the younger of the two.

"This factory makes the pots of gold for every rainbow in the whole world." Shamus said, proudly. "We're the managers you see. O'Leary's here's my deputy..."

53

"Hey, that's enough of your cheek." said O'Leary, "We're equal partners and you're not too old for a clip round the ear. "

"He's been saying that for t'ree hundred years," grumbled shamus. "Anyway... We are very grateful for your mammy's grand contribution to our workforce."

"You mean you do eat the cakes?" Daniel asked.

"Heavens no." said Shamus, "The cakes be sacred, lad."

As soon as he said that, Daniel felt very guilty for the occasional slice he had helped himself too. *Gulp*.

"I was going to get to that," smiled O'Leary "but it's a very delicate matter. The birth of a leprechaun requires..."

"The birth of a leprechaun...you mean the cakes are leprechaun eggs? Is my mum a leprechaun then? Does that make me a leprechaun?"

"Oh no no no." laughed Shamus "None of that. They're just an offering...to the new rainbows?"

"You mean you offer the rainbow a cake and it makes a leprechaun?" asked the now slightly calmer Daniel.

"That is the main sum of it." said O'Leary, "That's where we get the pots of gold too. Each is tied to its leprechaun keeper. The new leprechaun is created fully grown up I might add, usually beard and all. Me and Shamus here came from the same rainbow. That's how come we're brothers."

"The process takes a cracker of a cake." added Shamus "Rainbows have a very good sense of taste, you see. Luckily your mammy bakes like the sponge god herself." The little man gave a sigh of delight at the thought. "Only one in a generation can cook like that. Do you cook, me boy?" he asked.

"I've never really tried, actually." said Daniel, with embarrassment.

"Hmm," said Shamus "maybe you should."

"Would you look at that." smiled O'Leary, "Here comes a rainbow now."

"Where?" asked Daniel, looking round with excitement.

A huge and brilliant beam shone down over the whole central island. Daniel was bathed in its warm and friendly glow. The rainbow was sky blue, yellow and mint green, to name but a few colours.

"Hmm hum." coughed a deep and jolly woman's voice from nowhere. "You expect a mammy rainbow to create a new leprechaun without as much as a bite to eat?"

"Sorry me dear" said Shamus, apologetically, "We're a bit slow today aren't we? Showin' this young lad the place, you see. His name's Daniel."

"Just bring me the cake." said the rainbow, sharply. Then she softy added "Sorry Danny boy, but you gotta keep these boys on their toes."

"That's ok." smiled Daniel, "It's fantastic to meet a rainbow."

"Well I be thankin' you laddy." said the rainbow, merrily. "That be high praise from a baker's son. And here's one of yer mammy's master pieces now. And Yummy, yum yum, it looks good."

A group of three male and three, golden haired, female leprechauns came up from the factory floor. They were carrying a gigantic, pink, sparkling cake on a huge, golden plate. It had one golden candle burning on top. As soon as they entered the shaft of light a cool breeze somehow lifted the cake and set it floating in the centre of the beam. *Gobble, gobble, gobble* went the rainbow and giant bites magically disappeared here and there off of the cake, until it was all gone.

Daniel noticed some more leprechauns pushing a huge empty pot into the centre of the beam. Suddenly the leprechauns cheered joyfully as it began to rain down with thousands of four-leaf clovers. With a gentle jingling sound the pot was suddenly filled with beautiful, golden coins. On top of the pot sat a brand new leprechaun, dressed just like all the others. He looked like a chubby young man of about twenty with a rather stubbly face. The leprechauns all rushed in to shake the new fellow's hand. A parade of merrily singing workers carried him off onto the factory floor.

"That's that then." said the managers "Now let's have a little look about the place, shall we?"

Then the leprechauns showed Daniel all around the factory.

First they showed Daniel a huge golden trampoline called a Bounceagram. A huge mechanical arm, wearing a white glove would drop one pot of gold from the conveyer belt on to it at a time. The pot would bounce off onto another conveyer belt at the other side of the trampoline. There another mechanical arm would stamp it with its weight, number of coins and quality in carats. More often than not it was twenty four.

Then the leprechauns showed Daniel the great tumble tunnel. This was a huge, spinning, tube of pure gold the size of a train. It was lined with pink, candy floss like fluff. It spun at tremendous speeds. The conveyer belt would stop every few seconds and another of the huge mechanical hands would take a pot from the conveyer belt underneath the tumble tunnel. Its gold was poured into one end of the tube, which was slightly higher than the other. Then it would pour the brilliantly gleaming coins back into their pot at the other end of the tunnel. The leprechauns said that the pots were made of iron to ward of dark magic.

Then finally Daniel was taken deeper underground to the cataloguing and storage area. This was where the gold was kept at night. The leprechauns explained that it was best to keep the pots moving in the day or else their leprechauns would become awfully agitated and restless. Still, even in the day the enormous vault, lined with purest gold, instead of lead or steal was an impressive sight.

Daniel was astounded.

He, Shamus and O'Leary were just arriving back at the central island. They were going to conclude their tour with a few complimentary refreshments. Suddenly there was an enormous crash, then another and another.

"Quick, hide, me boy." Instructed the leprechauns and Daniel quickly took up position in a gap between some giant pots of gold.

About thirty giant sized, dark green trolls had smashed their way in through the roof. They were big, ugly, yellow nosed creatures in tatty brown cloths. They were climbing down from above at some speed, on ropes the thickness of tree trunks.

The leprechauns went crazy running about and trying to hide. O'Leary and Shamus ran for the office. Shamus quickly came back out holding some kind of chunky, golden pistol. He pointed it at the roof and was about to fire, when a troll knocked it out of his hands.

"Nooo!" cried Shamus as it went skittering across the floor. Shamus bit the troll several times and then tried to offer the troll a timeshare in his apartment on the Costa del Sol. I guess he thought it would calm the situation, but there was no reasoning with the troll. He smelt remarkably like a gorilla's deodorant free armpit. I just thought you'd like to know that.

"In you go." grunted the nasty creature, after receiving several more, sadly non toxic leprechaun bites.

He threw the heavily complaining Shamus in the office with his brother and blocked the door with one of the huge iron pots which the leprechauns used for gold.

"Ouch." cursed the great green beast, burning his fingers on the iron "Good riddance to bad leprechauns." he grumbled. The trolls had brought huge sacks with them and they began quickly loading them up with treasure. They were doing their best to ignore their slightly singed claws.

Daniel was horrified to see that leprechauns were being magically dragged into the bags with the gold. 'Of course.' he thought 'they're magically tied to it.'

"We're taking the gold." said all of the enormous trolls in one eerily ferocious growl. "Anyone who tries to stop us will be punished by a court of law and perhaps, then, just possibly, eaten just a little bit. Got it?"

There was a resounding *gulp* from the other leprechauns who all understood rather clearly. This was accompanied by the sound of trolls sucking their fingers and thumbs like great, green, grumbling babies. They probably needed a nappy change if their smell was anything to go by. This seemed to make them feel better and they continued looting. They still muttered the occasional "ouch."

The leprechaun workers all opted to try and hide as best as they could. They were powerless to stop the nasty old brutes anyway.

"I have to do something." Daniel thought to himself.

He panicked for a moment and then Daniel told himself firmly that he must think, very quickly. 'That golden pistol must do something useful,' he thought 'or shamus wouldn't have tried to fire it. He didn't even aim it at a troll'. Daniel had to get the gun but one of the giant brutes was in the way. Daniel gritted his teeth and ran. The troll quickly noticed Daniel and tried to grab hold of him. Luckily the beast was too slow for the swift young boy. Daniel slid right through the creatures legs, grabbed the gun and fired at the ceiling.

A giant ball of golden fire blasted out of the barrel, causing Daniel to stagger back. The blast escaped through one of the troll holes in the ceiling and then nothing...
The troll picked Daniel up in its huge, clawed hand.

"Yum yum yum." chanted the trolls.

Daniel was terrified.

Suddenly about fifty golden, glittering garden gnomes came sliding down the trolls' own ropes.

The trolls tried to grab the little fellows but these were very special creatures called Midas nomes. As the trolls made contact they just jingled to the ground, each turning into a huge pile of golden coins.

Daniel let the leprechaun managers out of the office. The very grateful little men rewarded him with a lovely tea party. They had golden biscuits, honeyed tea and a special surprise. For the first time ever, one of his mum's cakes was eaten in his honour.

"Me lad." said O'Leary. "I'm glad I nearly squashed ya, or we'd never have met the bravest and best friend in all the world."

"HERE HERE." cried a thousand leprechauns at once. Hundreds of glittering, truly golden eagles flew in through the troll holes in the roof. They circled above, gracefully and sung sweetly to the hero of the hour. Now that would probably explain the clanging, now wouldn't it? Metal birds, who would've thought it?

They all had a tremendous time. When the party was over, Daniel went home to begin a whole new adventure. He was going to ask his mum for cookery lessons, baking in particular...

The End

Smitten The Kitten and The Fairy Fun Fair

Smitten awoke bright and early. Today was the day. The day the fair came to town. Posters had been plastered all over Fuzzelhill for weeks. All of the town's children were so excited, but none as much as Smitten.

He literally jumped out of bed, already wearing his favourite blue cardigan and yellow shorts. He ran to the bathroom to brush his teeth. Before he left, he had a feeling that he should take his lucky whistle with him. It had been enchanted by a brush with a powerful wizard and now had the power to grant the occasional wish. Smitten didn't use it very often. He thought that the magic had to run out some time. It had only got enchanted by accident. He ran back into his room and grabbed it off of his bedside table.

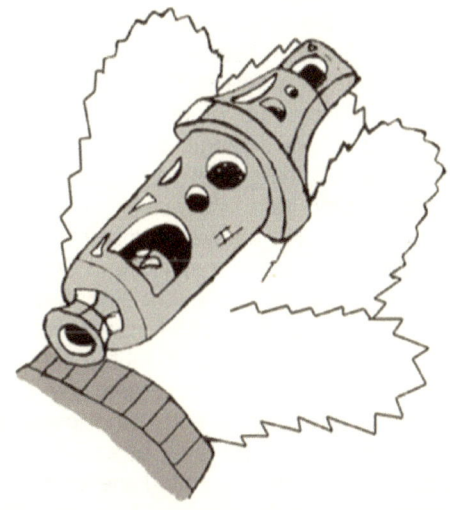

"Got ya." he said to himself.

Then he ran downstairs.

"Mornin' mum." he said to the chubby older cat woman. She wore a pink dress with yellow spots.

"Morning son." she smiled, "Isn't it that thingy today? You know? The fair."

"Yeh mum." said Smitten, "Gotta dash. I wanna be the first one there."

"Ok," said his mother, "I under..." he zoomed past her, grabbing a slice of toast off the table. Then he was gone out the door. "...stand." She finished "Oh... Bye." she said. Then she sat down for a cup of tea.

Smitten raced through the streets of Fuzzlehill, knocking people's elbows all the way. He overtook all the other children on their way to the fairground. When he arrived on the common, he was not disappointed. The fair looked amazing.

There was a big wheel, a carousel with wooden animals to ride and even a little rollercoaster. There were also a number of small colourful tents of blue and yellow, scattered about the place.

Smitten rode on the big wheel and had a great time on the carousel with the other kids. They all liked pretending they were having races on real horses and not the wooden ones. Then he went for a ride on the rollercoaster. Now this was great too but from his higher point of view smitten noticed something rather strange. Not fifty feet away from the fairground it was raining. Not raining just a little bit, but heavy rain, really heavy rain. 'Why ain't it rainin' here then?' he thought, to himself. He allowed himself to enjoy the rest of the ride, even letting out a merry shout or two. When he got off of the ride he decided to take a bit of a walk round the fairground. He wanted to find out what was going on. There didn't seem to be any harm about it. All the kids were having a great time. They were screaming with joy on the rides, eating ice-creams and candy floss and generally having great fun. Looking round, Smitten's attention was drawn to the fairground folk that were running the place. There was something about them that niggled at him, but what? Then it hit him. None of them were any taller than the children. And they all had rather pointed ears, didn't they? Smitten whistled, casually as he moved closer to one of them, to get a better look. Their skin seemed to have a slight tint of green and this particular woman looked rather delicate.

Then he heard a voice calling him.

"Young man." called the old woman, from inside the tent beside him.

He looked at her.

"Me?" he asked.

"Yes you, the Kitten lad. Come here. I sense something regarding your personal safety."

Smitten was confused for a second, until he looked up. The sign on the tent read 'Fortune Teller'. Smitten didn't believe in fortune tellers. Did he? He gulped and stepped inside the tent.

"Hello." said the old lady. She was sitting by a table with a crystal ball. "Have a seat."

So smitten sat down opposite the lady, noticing her pointy ears sticking out from under her head scarf. She was dressed in a rich red gown with long baggy sleeves. She also wore large, golden earrings.

"Ello." said Smitten, nervously, "what did you...uh...want to talk to me about? I ain't done nothin'. Honest I ain't."

"Ah." said the woman, wisely, "It's not what has been done that is the problem. It is the future, your personal future. I see grave danger, very soon, today in fact. It is almost upon you now?"

"How do you know?" asked Smitten, with a gulp.

The crystal ball began to glow with bright, white swirls, like a ball of living mist.

"Ah." said Smitten. "If you don't mind, I'll be going home now."

"I fear it may be too late for that." said the woman, wisely, "but by all means try. Good luck, my boy."

Smitten got up and ran. He moved even more swiftly than the way he had arrived. Sadly, it did indeed seem too late. As soon as Smitten had gotten clear of the fairground tents and rides, he hit some kind of invisible, magic barrier. The kitten bounced off it, as if he had hit a trampoline. After landing on his bottom on the thankfully soft grass, he got back up, swiftly.

"Good job I brought this." he said, rifling through his pockets and taking out the whistle. There were other children trying to leave now. They were all bouncing off the barrier too. Everyone started to panic and run about all over the place.

Smitten put the whistle to his lips and blew, loudly.

He wished with all his might that the magical barrier would come down and that they would all be able to leave. As he tried to run through it again he just bounced off once more. 'Why ain't it workin?" he said. Smitten was rather puzzled.

Then his question was answered. A loud voice came on over the fairground loud speaker system.

"On behalf of all fairy fairground staff," said the voice.

'So they're fairies.' thought smitten. 'Magic must be hiding their wings.'

The speaker continued.

"I would like to inform you of our situation."

'Situation?' thought Smitten.

"There is a dark fairy somewhere within the fairground. And due to this we have had to lock down the premises. Sorry for any inconvenience caused. Also, just a note for the kitten, all unauthorised magical items have been disabled until further notice. Thank you."

"Cheeky blighters." Smitten said to himself.

Then a team of six fairies ran passed him, dressed in black. Their yellow, petal like wings were no longer hidden. They looked like security guards. 'They must be looking for the bad guy.' thought smitten.

He knew he'd been warned about danger but he thought that the bad guy's magic must have been disabled too. Smitten began searching round the fairground, looking for the dark intruder. He thought he would use his magicless whistle to call for help, if he needed it.

To calm the other children down, there were fairies handing out free ice cream. This made searching a little easier. Smitten checked around all of the rides and even inside the tents. He found no dark fairies but then he noticed a very small tent, which he had neglected to check. It was right near the fairground's entrance. He made his way over and poked his head inside. 'Nothing' he thought, so he stood by the doorway and looked out at the fairground. Suddenly Smitten froze, he heard someone moving, behind him, in the tent. They must have been hiding when he'd looked. 'Wait a minute' thought smitten, 'why would they be hiding now? Unless... It must be..."

Smitten leapt round and grabbed the fairy man by the arm. The fairy yelled at him and turned to face him, with magically glowing hands.

"Let go". The evil creature commanded him but Smitten took his whistle and blew. The darkly dressed fairy growled and the glow spread to the rest of his body. Then smitten found himself glowing too. He felt very weak as he fell to the floor.

Then smitten woke up. Or did he? He was standing in a bright yellow maze, with a swirling floor of blue and green. The sky was blue and cloudless

"Where am I?" he asked himself. He wondered around for what seemed like hours. He was hopelessly lost. He met someone every now again. They were all dressed in colourful clothes but would never face him or speak. He was soon ready to give up. He could just sit there pretty much forever. But then he heard a familiar voice. "Smitten, don't do that. Follow me."

A floating, green balloon appeared in front of him, on a string. It wore a pair of thick, round framed glasses.

"I can't," he told the balloon "I'm too tired."

"Nonsense" said the balloon.

It wrapped its string round his paw and began pulling him through the maze. Smitten kept trying to resist, but it was of no use. This balloon was very strong. Finally Smitten found himself right in the centre of the maze.

'I thought you were leading me out?" he said, sleepily.

"I am." replied the balloon. It swelled to the size of an elephant and lifted him up into the sky.

Smitten woke up to find his friend Henrietta, the plump hamster witch, standing over him. She was dressed in her usual green dress, and thick round rimmed spectacles.

"Hello." she said "I'm glad that you're back. I had to use a very powerful spell to guide you home."

"Why were you a bloomin' balloon?" asked smitten. "Couldn't you have been a hedge cutter? Wouldn't that have got through quicker?"

"You do not need to tell me about your dream, Smitten." said Henrietta. "That is only yours to know. I merely reached in to pull you out. Your mind decided how."

Smitten looked round to see that the dark fairy was being led away in hand cuffs by the fairy security people. One of them walked over and said.

"I must thank you for blowing your whistle so we could find the intruder. Its magic will work again now. I sense that its power is low so I would not use it often. "

"Who is that nasty fairy?" asked Smitten, getting up. "And why did his magic still work when mine didn't?"

"His name is Phillip Thunderfox." said the security guard "He was able to keep both himself and his powers hidden by dark trickery. Thunderfox is a wanted felon who can now be dealt with, thanks to you, my boy."

The fairy shook his hand and left.

"How did you get in?" asked Smitten.

"As soon as you blew the whistle they caught him." said Henrietta, with a smile "Then they took down the barrier. I had sensed your trouble and was waiting outside. You were only out for a few minutes but it was touch and go. We could have lost you. I'm so glad we didn't."

"Well," said Smitten, rubbing his sore head. "I think I've had enough of the fairground for one day. I think I'll go home and have a proper breakfast...

The End

Moona and The Talent Show

It was a warm summer's day and Moona the cow was in the village shop. She was picking up a few bits and pieces for the farmer. That was when she saw it. Behind the counter was a notice that read "Village Talent show. All acts welcome. "

"Wow." Moona said to Mrs Jones the shop keeper, "I'm a very talented cow. I could enter that."

"What a wonderful, exciting thing to do, my dear." said Mrs Jones, with a smile "What will you perform then? You'll have to be ready for this afternoon."

"This afternoon." gasped Moona.

Then she thought about it. "Well" she said. "I have been practicing my martial arts. I could do a cow-foo demonstration."

"Very good." said Mrs Jones. "That sounds like fun to watch."

"But," said Moona, as if asking a question "I'll need a partner......."

"Oh, not me, my dear," laughed Mrs Jones. "I'm getting a bit old for things like that."

Then she shouted out "Burn?"

Her son, Burney, the gangly, spotted youth came through from out back, picking his nose.

"What is it ma?" he asked.

His mum opened her mouth to speak, but Moona cut her off.

"Nothing Burn, it doesn't matter."

She didn't think burn would be much use in a martial arts act.

He shrugged and walked back out the door.

"Don't you want to enter any more?" Mrs Jones asked Moona.

"I think," said Moona, "that I'm going to have to give it a bit more thought."

Moona headed off back to the farm. On her way she met Phillip the fox. He was waiting for someone at the road side.

"How do you fancy doing a martial arts act with me at the talent show?" said Moona.

"Sorry Moona," said Phillip, "I'm already doing a dance act."

"Oh," said Moona, "that sounds like fun. I'm a great dancer. Can I join your act?"

"Sorry to say it," replied Phillip, "but I've already got a partner."

His sister Phoebe the fox pranced up to them, in a pink tutu.

"Hi Moona," she said, with a twirl "Phillip, are you ready to practice?"

Yep he replied, and they pranced off together.

So Moona carried on walking. As she crossed a grassy meadow she met Shannon the sheep.

"Hi Shannon," said Moona "would you like to join my martial arts act for the talent show?"

"Baaaa." replied the sheep, "Can't, Moona. I'm already entering."

"Oh," replied Moona, "what's your act then?"

"Me and the rest of the flock are doing a clown act. Little cars, Stuff like that."

"Ok," said Moona, "sounds like great fun. Can I join?"

"Sorry Moona," said Shannon. "I don't think you'd fit in the cars."

"Ok," said Moona "that's alright. "I'm sure the farmer will join my act."

When Moona reached the farm, she went straight in to see farmer John. He was sat at the table eating his lunch.

She put his shopping down on the table.

"Hello, Moona." he said with a smile. "Thanks for getting my shopping."

"That's ok," said Moona, smiling sweetly "Do you think you could do me a favour?"

"Anything for you, my dear." the farmer replied.

"Join my martial arts act? Please."

"For this afternoon's talent show?" asked the farmer.

"Yes John," said Moona, fluttering her eyelids "would you?"

"If it were anything else, my dear, I would do," said the farmer, sadly "but I'm afraid I just got a last minute phone call. I'm on the judging panel. I can't enter."

"Oh no." said Moona, with a sob, "What can I do?" I can't enter on my own."

"Why not?" asked the farmer, "Your cow- foo is very good. I'm sure you'd do fine."

Moona shook her head. "I just couldn't. I'd be far too nervous. I'll just have to sit back and watch everyone else have fun."

"If that's how you feel, Moona." said farmer John, getting up and placing a reassuring hand on her shoulder. "You don't really have to go."

"No," sighed Moona, "I wouldn't want to miss out completely."

She went out to the barn and painted her toenails pink. She wanted to look her best. Shortly after that she and farmer john drove into town in his four by four. They went inside the crowded town hall. Farmer John gave her a pat on the back. Then he went and sat with the other judges at the front of the room. Moona took a seat at the back of the crowd.

She watched the sheep in their little clown cars get straight sevens out of ten. Then she watched the dancing foxes score brilliantly too. Their ballet was top class. She expected they'd score perfectly. But in fact they got nine out of ten from everyone. She watched about ten more acts. Some were really good. But she would be surprised if anyone beat the foxes. Then came the real surprise.

Burn Jones took the stage, dressed in his red kung-foo robes. Moona was stunned. He announced out loud that he was about to do a martial arts demonstration. She felt guilty for not asking him to join her. This was her reward. He would do it without her.

Burn took his position at centre stage. He was about to begin, when he saw Moona at the back of the hall. She looked very upset. Then he gave a sigh and called out,

"Moona, how would you like to join me?"

"Really? " gasped Moona.

"Really." said Burn.

She ran up to the stage and took her position at his side. Following Burn's lead she and Burn gave the most spectacular cow-foo and kung-foo demonstration ever. When the judges held up their cards it was ten out of ten all round.

They stood together in centre stage as the smiling farmer John presented them with their new, shiny, golden medals. Moona secretly hoped that hers was chocolate.

"I wasn't doing the demonstration to upset you, Moona." said Burn. "When mum told me about you doing yours I had already planned mine. I'm surprised she didn't tell you."

"I don't think I gave her a chance." said Moona, guiltily. "I'm so sorry. I didn't think you looked like a..."

"Like a martial arts sort of lad." Burn finished. "I agree," he said, with a smile "without the uniform I don't. But you really should look deeper than the way people look."

Moona nodded. "I will next time. I promise."

"Ok," said Burn, "I forgive you. Now let's wave to the crowd...

The End

Lee Pritchett

The Mystery of The Bonfire Ghost

It was a beautiful, starlit night this November the fifth. Ginger haired, twelve- year-old Harry Bundlesnoop and his eleven-year-old best friend Eliza were headed for the old castle of Lord Buglehorn. He was the wealthy nobleman who had ruled Hillington town, hundreds of years ago.

"I can't wait for the fireworks." said Harry "The paper said this year they're going to be the best they've ever put on. Rockets, catherine wheels, the whole kit and caboodle."

"Well." said Eliza "I hope it lives up to all the hype. Let's get a move on."

The two friends made their way up the lantern lit hillside road. Lots of other people were also doing the same.

They were headed up to the hilltop, outside the castle wall, where the bonfire had already been lit. In precisely thirty minutes the fireworks display would begin.

When they arrived, Harry and Eliza were met by a huge gathering. It was busier than any event they had ever seen in their quiet little town. Everybody was wrapped up warm, including Harry and Eliza. Harry wore a big, thick red jacket, with a yellow scarf. Eliza wore a puffy yellow coat with a white fluffy collar, and a pink bobble hat on top of her long, blonde hair.

Everyone was crowded round the huge bonfire and the younger children were getting ready to put their Guy Fawkes's on the flames.

Just by co-incidence Harry happened to glance down into the castle moat. What he saw frightened him. The ghostly white figure was dressed in the pure white robes and wide brimmed hat of an ancient musketeer.

He turned to Eliza and whispered in her ear, so as not to sound too mad.

"There's a ghost, Eliza, Down in the moat."

"What?" she replied, loudly "Did you say a ghost?"

"Talk quietly," he told her "or everyone's going to think I've gone nuts. Just look for yourself." He pointed down to the moat and she did indeed look.

"There's nothing there." she told him, seeming amused.

"It's not funny." he told her "There was something there a moment ago."

"Ok," said Eliza "I believe you."

She smiled a little too much for him to take her seriously.

"Ok," he said, "I'll prove it too you. Come with me." He took her hand and led her towards a little path that meandered its way down into the grassy moat.

"Are you sure we should do this?" said Eliza, with concern. "There's not long 'till the fireworks start, and even if there is a ghost, do we really want to meet it, face to face?"

"We'll be fine." said Harry, sounding like he was now enjoying himself on their ghost hunt. "We'll take a quick look and be back in ten minutes, maybe with an amazing story to tell."

"Ten minutes?" said Eliza "You promise?"

"Definitely," said Harry, "promise."

A moment later they were down in the bottom of the moat, cautiously making their way along in the now slightly eerie moonlight.

Just then Eliza spotted something. "There," she said "up ahead. I saw it. Let's turn back now." She sounded a little scared.

"I see it too." said Harry, then it suddenly disappeared. "Come on," he said "I want to see it up close. A real ghost, how exciting."

"I'm going back." said Eliza. Then she turned to go.

"Do you really want to walk back on your own?" said Harry.

"Hmmm." said Eliza.

Suddenly a huge, eerie white bird swooped them from above.

The two children jumped, but then they laughed.

"It was just a barn owl." they said together.

"Ok," said Harry "I guess my eyes were playing tricks on me and making it took like a man. Let's head back."

Just then they saw it again, closer this time and it definitely wasn't an owl.

The ghostly figure was now running towards them, waving something in the air, two somethings.

"Ahhh," Eliza cried. She turned and ran, but Harry just stood there and watched the man approach.

"Elisa," he called "It's just a...." but she couldn't hear him.

Eliza arrived back at the bonfire, acting like a mad woman. "You have to help me." she said to a man "There's a ghost down in the moat and it's got my friend."

"Calm down, love." said the man. "Who've you lost? That lad I just saw you with, a moment ago?"

"Yes." said Eliza.

"You mean the one standing behind you, eating a toffee apple, with a bloke in white?"

Eliza turned and nearly passed out with shock. "What on earth?" she said "You mean he's............?"

"Just a man." said the musketeer. "I'm doing a publicity stunt for the council. They reckoned havin' a ghost sneakin' about would help the atmosphere tonight."

"I don't believe it." gasped Eliza,

"We get a free toffee apple each, for finding him first." said Harry.

Then she accepted hers, gratefully. She thought the sugar might help with the shock.

Then Harry and Eliza watched a terrific, moonlit fireworks display, together on the castle hilltop. They knew they'd remember this night for the rest of their lives...

The End

The Land of Buttons and Milk

Sally bear was big, cuddly teddy that lived in the bedroom of a sweet little six-year-old girl called Joanne. The bear was in fact nearly as big as the girl and they went everywhere together. Sally bear always wore her favourite, pink dungarees with yellow buttons on the shoulder straps.

As you would expect, Sally bear could in fact both walk and talk, but no-one else knew this. For some reason Sally bear had never met another toy that could, but she knew she couldn't be the only one. Could she?

One morning Sally bear woke up to quite a surprise. It was only seven thirty in the morning and she was all alone in Joanne's bedroom.

"I wonder where Joanne's got to." Sally bear said to herself, getting up and straightening her dungarees. She climbed out from among the other teddies and had a good look round the room, just to make sure that she wasn't in fact mistaken. She even checked under the bed and then had a good bounce on top of it to make doubly sure. But there was no Joanne.

She checked mum and dad's room and then downstairs but there was no sign of anybody.

"Where are they?" she asked herself. She looked out of the window and the family car was still in the drive. 'Hmmm." she thought. Then she went out in the back garden and even had a good poke around in all the hedges, before finally checking the shed.

When she opened the door, Sally bear got a huge surprise. "Wow." she said. There was a huge whirlpool of bright purple energy filling up the floor of the room. "I wonder what it is?" said Sally bear. Then she suddenly found her feet being pulled towards the whirlpool. She tried to fight it but the pull was too strong. Sally bear was sucked into the portal and found herself spiralling downwards, into a tunnel of purple energy.

A few moments later, she found herself landing with a soft thud, on very furry ground. There was no sign of the portal from this end. The green fur on the ground appeared to be some kind of grass, but made out of soft furry felt.

Around her were small fluffy trees, made out of a similar material to the ground. They were covered in large, golden buttons.

Sally picked one and discovered it was actually covered in shiny, golden foil. Sally peeled off the covering and found something very welcome inside. She was holding a giant chocolate button and she had not in fact had breakfast. She gobbled it down gratefully then went for a walk.

Soon she found herself standing on the edge of a milky white lake. Sally was thirsty so leaned down for a drink, finding it to actually be milk, Sally bear's favourite drink.

"Mmm." she said.

Then she noticed that there was someone fishing on the far banks of the lake. "HELLO." she called "CAN YOU HELP ME?" since she was in a strange world, she imagined it didn't really matter if anyone heard her talk. When she went home, if she went home, she would never see them again.

The fisherman didn't seem to hear her, so sally began walking round the lake to get closer. When she got there she was quite surprised by who she found. The fisherman was in fact another teddy bear, almost identical to herself but wearing blue dungarees, instead of pink. And he was listening to a personal stereo.

"Hello." he said, taking out his earphones. "Lovely day, isn't it?"

"You're...you're..." Sally bear stuttered "you're just like me."

"Not quite." said the teddy, sounding insulted. "I'm a boy and you're a girl. That's the second time I've been insulted today."

"Who else insulted you?" asked Sally bear, thinking insulted was a bit of a strong word.

"The three humans that came through here about an hour ago." said the bear "Didn't you see 'em?"

"Three humans." gasped Sally "A little girl and her parents?"

"Could have been." said the bear "One was much smaller than the other two."

"That's my family." said Sally bear "Which way did they go?"

"Your family?" asked the confused Teddy "But you're a bear."

"I've lived with them for as long as I can remember." she replied "and I love them very much. They're my family."

"Ok." said the bear, still looking confused "They went that way, into town."

He pointed towards a huddled group of red, yellow, and blue, fluffy buildings in the distance.

So off sally bear went to find her family.

Soon she was walking in amongst the buildings. The streets were paved with big, rectangular lolly pops of pink, yellow, blue and lots of other colours.

Sally was greatly surprised when a group of ten teddies came up to her. Some were dressed in blue, some yellow and some were in pink, like her.

"Come to our party. " they said "Please will you come to our party?"

"I'd love to." said Sally bear, "but I have to find my family."

"I'm sure they'll be at the party." said a bear in pink. "Everyone will be."

"But I don't think..." began Sally bear, but the teddies weren't taking no for an answer and ushered her over to the largest building in town. It was a huge, fluffy yellow cube, with little, square, coloured windows, like the lollipops on the ground.

When she got inside there were about a hundred teddy bears but no sign of her family.

"Why are there so many talking teddy bears here?" Sally bear asked one of them. "Until today I was afraid there was only me?"

"Where have you been then?" asked the boy teddy, dressed in blue. "This is the land of buttons and milk. This is where we live, where we all come from."

"You mean I come from here?" she gasped.

"Of course." said the bear. "Where else would a talking teddy come from?"

"I live with the humans?" she told him.

"On earth?" he asked "I heard the food's awful there. Why don't you come back and live with us?"

'Hmmm.' thought Sally bear.

One of the bears brought her a drink of milk and she had a bit of a dance, but then the door to the hall opened again and in walked three humans.

It was a little girl with blond pig tails and glasses, wearing her blue and white chequered school dress. She was accompanied by her mum and dad.

"JO JO." cried Sally bear. She ran over and hugged her, tightly.

"Do I know you?" said Joanne.

"Know me?" said Sally bear, sounding rather worried "It's me, Sally bear."

"Sally bear?" gasped Joanne. "You can talk too?"

"Sorry I had to keep it a secret," said Sally bear "but I was the only one back home. Here there's lots of us and I never even knew."

"I knew." said dad, trying to sound clever.

"No you didn't." said mum, clipping him round the ear.

"Oww." he said "But I did." so she did it again.

"No, I didn't." he admitted and walked off to get a drink of milk.

"I'm so pleased you found your family." said mum, with a semi-smile. She knew Joanne would be very upset to lose her if she stayed.

Joanne looked sad.

"But...but." said Sally bear "*You're* my family."

"You mean it?" gasped Joanne. "You'll stay with me and be my friend, like you always have been, sisters?"

"Of course." said Sally bear.

Joanne, Sally bear and mum shared another big hug.

Then a bear in blue dungarees with a hint of a wispy grey beard came up to them.

"My dear Sally bear." he said "I'm so glad you're happy and you made the right decision."

Sally bear had a funny feeling about this bear. "Do I know you?" she asked.

"Indeed you do." he said with a smile "I'm your father."

"My father?" gasped Sally and with that he conjured a small, silver button out of mid air.

"Yes." he said "You asked me to wipe your memory with my magic five years ago."

"Why?" she asked.

"You said you had been to earth and found a very special girl who needed you. So you went to live with her. Now, are you sure you don't want to come back?"

Sally bear thought for a moment.

He handed her the silver button. "If you ever do or you just want to visit, throw this on the ground and say 'Teddy dum num', ok?"

"Oh daddy." she said, giving him a big hug "Thank you so much for everything. I will come and visit, but me and Joanne still very much need each other.

"Ok, my dear." he said with a smile. "It's been so nice to see you."

Joanne gave him a big hug too. Then he gave them each a giant chocolate tree button to take home and in a clap of his hands, Sally found herself back among the toys in Joanne's bedroom.

"Was it a dream?" she thought. Then Joanne came running in holding her giant tree button. She picked up Sally bear, gave her a huge hug and swung her around. "I love you, Sally bear." she said, with tears of joy.

"I love you too." said Sally bear. And they both laughed out loud.

The End

Lee Pritchett

Holly and The Winter Match

One snowy day, little Holly decided to go for a walk in the woods behind her parents' house. She put on a big, fluffy, pink coat, a red woolly hat and her favourite purple wellington boots.

When she jumped over the little garden fence, Holly was amazed at just how snowy it was in the wood.

She walked on through the forest for a little while without seeing any sign of the woodland animals.

'I wonder where everyone is?' she thought to herself.

But then she heard something, the sound of jolly music playing on the wind.

Holly followed the sound and soon came to a part of the woodland she had never seen before. It was a huge clearing containing a massive frozen lake. Skating on the lake were all of the woodlanders. There was the water rat, the dear and her kung-foo fawn, Berty the little unicorn in his little blue bobble hat, and his mother in her pink tutu. Even the brown bear was there in his long, red woolly scarf. He was playing the jolly melody on his flute whilst the others merrily skated around him.

"Hello, everyone." called Holly and they all rushed over to greet their friend.

"Hello Holly." said Berty "We're having our yearly Christmas party. So glad you could make it."

"A Christmas party?" asked Holly, "Why didn't you invite me? I love parties."

"What do you mean?" asked the mother unicorn. "We did. Mr Water rat dropped round your invitation weeks ago, didn't he?"

The water rat, rather embarrassingly took a piece of paper out of the pocket of his little, yellow coat and handed it to Holly. "Eh...Sorry about the delay, but I got there in the end."

Holly gave him a stern look and said "Well, I suppose you're right. At least I'm here now."

"Just in time to meet our special guest." said the kung-foo fawn, who was wearing red earmuffs and a yellow scarf.

He did a very acrobatic back flip and the bear played a loud salute as a tiny penguin came darting towards them out of no-where from the other side of the lake.

He made a huge shower of ice spray through the air as he stopped at their side.

The penguin wore a little red Santa hat with a green bobble.

"This is Unwin the penguin," said the mother dear "our special winter friend."

"Nice to meet you." said Unwin, with a big smile. "Don't worry, Holly, I have a present for you too."

"A present?" asked Hollie "Why would you bring me a present? We've never even met."

"I brought presents for everyone in the wood." said the Unwin "Just like I do every year. Santa likes it that way."

"You know Santa Clause?" gasped Holly.

"He's a good friend," said Unwin "and he speaks very highly of you. You're one of his favourites."

"Really?" asked Holly "Me?"

"Yes," said the penguin. "All of you are, just because you're such good friends to each other. So this year I have a very special present for all of you to share."

"Share?" asked the kung-foo fawn, sounding disappointed. "But...?"

"No buts," said his mum "just say thank you to the nice penguin."

"Oh...thank you." said the fawn, sounding glum.

"You'll all love it," said the penguin, with a smile. "I assure you. We're going to have a Christmas game of ice hockey and the winners get a very special prize."

"Ok," said Holly, "That sounds fun." and everyone agreed. "But I haven't got any skates." she said, glumly.

"It's ok," said the Penguin "I have an old pair you can borrow."

He handed them over. They were brown and tatty, but she was happy just to have some skates at all.

"Oh, thank you." she said, smiling politely.

The brown bear, who was wearing a long, red scarf, handed out some hockey sticks, while the penguin set up the goals.

"I'm going to give it a miss, if you don't mind." said the brown bear, patting Unwin on the back.

Everyone was shocked. Then the bear explained why.

"This game is a present from Santa," he told them "but my music is a present from me. I want to keep playing it for you all whilst you play hockey. I think it will be more special that way."

Everyone smiled.

"Thank you so much." They all said together and everyone gave him a big hug.

"I'm going to be the umpire." said the Penguin "That way teams are even."

Holly, Berty and his mum were on one team. The kung-foo fawn, his mum and the water rat were on the other team.

As the game got going it seemed clear the martial arts trained deer and the agile water rat had an advantage. They scored goal after goal. Berty's mum was a graceful ballerina but Holly wasn't used to skating and Berty was a bit clumsy on the ice to be honest. He kept tripping up and losing his bobble hat.

At half time, Holly's team huddled for a talk. "We need to do better." said Holly, sounding worried.

Berty agreed. "If we lose, we don't get our presents."

"It's not about winning, dear." said his mum "It's about the taking part."

The children had of course heard this before but at the present moment they were having a hard time taking it in. "Honestly," said the mother Unicorn "just have fun. That's what's important."

Holly and Berty took no notice. In the next half they tried with all their might to score some goals, but they just couldn't. Berty started to cry. "Oh mummy, Holly," he said "we're losing so badly, my clumsy feet have let you all down."

"Don't say that, Berty." his mother told him.

"You haven't let us down, Berty." said Holly. "You've tried your best. I'm no ballerina on the ice either, not like your mum. She'd probably have a hundred goals by now without me getting in the way."

"Nonsense, Holly," said the mother Unicorn. "It's not about scoring goals. Look at the other team."

When Holly and Berty did so they noticed something. The other side weren't dead set on winning. They weren't fixed on the game, like her and Berty. They were just laughing, playing and having fun.

"Let's Play." Holly and Berty said, with a grin.

The rest of the game was brilliant. They laughed and joked and had such fun, just enjoying the game so that winning didn't matter anymore. They did even manage to score a few goals.

"Well Holly," said the Penguin at the end of the game. "I'm sorry you didn't win, but now I have to present the prizes.

Holly felt a little glum again at this point.

The little penguin fetched a big sack out from behind a tree. He gave everyone on the other team a present. Then Holly's team got a lovely surprise when he also handed one to each of them.

"You're all winners" he said, giving each of them a hug. "It's the playing the game that counts and you all played it brilliantly..."

"Wow," said Holly "thank you so much. This is the best Christmas party I've ever been to. She gave Unwin a big hug and then they all unwrapped their presents.

All of the animals got a stuffed toy that looked just like them. The toys were all dressed in a red jumper, Santa hat, and tiny little ice skates. But Holly got something different and very special. A brand new pair of real, pink, sparkly ice skates, so she had some all of her own.

"These are amazing." she gasped "This is the best present ever. WOO HOO." she shouted, jumping with joy. She put them on right away and had a quick skate about before they all had Christmas cake and hot chocolate with marshmallows.

The bear, secretly feeling rather disappointed, played on as everyone celebrated. Then the penguin came up to him and offered one final package.

"A present, for me?" he asked, excitedly.

"Yes." said the Penguin "You didn't think Santa had forgotten you, did you? You're just as special as everyone else and you've played such lovely music for us all. Take it. You deserve it.

The bear gratefully accepted his present. It was long and thin and when he opened it, he found something fantastic.

"A clarinet." he gasped "A beautiful, red clarinet. How did you know I wanted a new instrument to play on?"

"Santa knows everything." said the Penguin, with a wink.

The bear picked him up and gave him a huge hug, swinging him round. Then he had a thought.

"What about you?" he asked.

"Me?" asked Unwin, sounding surprised "I got to hear your beautiful music, just like everyone else. That's more than enough."

The bear held out his shiny silver flute and said "Take this."

"I couldn't do that." gasped the penguin. "It's my job to give presents, not take from people."

"You're not taking." said the bear, with a smile. "I'm giving and I want you to have it."

"But I can't play." said the penguin, looking embarrassed about this.

"It's fun to learn something new." said the bear "Go on, take it, you deserve it."

The penguin bowed and graciously accepted the gift.

"Thank you." he said.

"Aw," said Holly "how sweet."

The bear played on his new instrument and they all skated, danced and drank hot chocolate till they were getting sleepy and it was time to go home. What a lovely Christmas party, with fun, food and good friends....

The End

Lucy and The Christmas Bear

It was particularly windy this Christmas Eve. As little Lucy looked out of her bedroom window the sun was setting over the snowy hills. She was dressed in her favourite pink nighty and pyjamas. Her long, golden pig tales dangled down over her shoulders. Lucy hadn't seen many Christmases. In fact this was only number seven in her personal Christmas count. The first few of which she couldn't even remember. But she thought that there was something particularly special about this Christmas. She had a tingly feeling in her toes, and Lucy's toes never let her down.

Lucy's mum came in and tucked her in tightly, and gave her a kiss goodnight. Then the happy little girl drifted off to sleep. She dreamed of the Thundergirls pink princess catapult. She had seen it in the village shop that very day. She would love it for Christmas, but it had been too late to ask.

Suddenly, at around midnight, Lucy woke up to the loud sound of shattering glass. It was the window. Something the size of a large cuddly toy came crashing through it. Lucy jumped up and screeched out loud.

"MUM."

But strangely, no-one came.

Lucy slowly got up and slipped on her pink bunny slippers. Then she walked over to the doorway and switched on the light.

"Could I trouble you for a cup of coco?" said a tiny little bear in a red Father Christmas suit. He wore a small, silver, star shaped badge on his breast pocket. "It's awfully cold in here with that window open." he wasn't a toy and was in fact quite real. He was a miniature, fully grown adult bear.

"Hello." said the stunned Lucy. "Who are you?"

"I'm the Christmas bear." he replied, cheerily, "Made a bit of a crash landing I'm afraid? Sorry about that. At least I got here eh?"

"How did you get here?" asked Lucy, intrigued. "It's almost as if you flew."

"I did." replied the bear, "In my magical rubber ring."

"In a rubber ring?" asked Lucy, quite confused.

"Yes." said the bear, matter-of-factly. "What's strange about that? Honestly, you humans have got some strange ideas. Last year this one boy told me that you're meant to eat brussel sprouts. A sweet lad, but not too bright."

"What are you supposed to do with them then?" ask Lucy, with confusion.

"Haven't you ever heard of sprout bowling?" asked the equally stunned bear.

"No," replied Lucy "but I have played skittles with my friends."

The bear sighed, deeply.

"It's no fun without the sprouts...Anyway I think we should get going."

"Where to?" asked Lucy.

"Santa's workshop, of course." replied the bear. "You're expected. And besides we've got a dragon to deal with."

"A dragon?" gasped Lucy.

"Yep." replied the bear, "What did you think knocked me out of the sky. He took my rubber ring you know."

"But why?" asked Lucy, "What good is a tiny rubber ring to a huge dragon?"

"It's my key to the workshop." The bear replied, "All the workers have one. With it he can get inside and take all the presents for himself."

"The nasty old fellow." said Lucy, "But what did you mean about me being expected?"

"You're one of the chosen few." said the bear. "You've been invited to Santa's Christmas eve tea party. If there still is one, with the dragon and all. We had better get going."

"But if you flew here in your rubber ring," asked Lucy, "then how do we get to the workshop without it?"

"Ahh," replied the bear, wisely "that's easy."

He whistled and a little, fluffy cloud came rushing in through the window. It panted away happily, just like a dog."

"By snow cloud of course." said the bear, with a big grin.

Lucy grabbed a warm, red coat from her wardrobe. She and the bear sat on the little cloud, cross legged. Then they were off out the window, into the star filled, midnight sky. They zoomed up high above the other clouds and their ride left a snowy trail behind them in the moonlight.

They travelled at amazing speeds, over land, sea and ice. In what seemed like no time at all, they arrived at the North Pole.

The cloud was now huffing and puffing, with exhaustion.

"I don't know," said the bear, with a sigh "these British snow clouds aren't up to much. One good flurry and they're done. "

Santa's workshop looked very much like a huge, donut shaped toy shop. There was a huge, glowing sign on the front that read 'Ho ho ho.' in big, red letters. The building was covered in icicles and was decorated in bright red and green. Giant model reindeer, the size of elephants moved on a train track around a giant hole in the roof.

As they moved towards the opening, the bear spoke,

"This is the way Father Christmas takes his reindeer in and out of the workshop."

As they looked inside, it appeared that Santa had an unwanted visitor. He and the elves did not look pleased at all, to say the least.

A huge, purple dragon was sat in the middle of the workshop on an enormous pile of colourful Christmas presents. He wore a red Santa hat. Most of the frightened elves were running around frantically, screaming "Santa! Santa!" Some looked stunned, staring at the sight in front of them.

"Oh no." gasped Lucy.

"It's worse than I thought." said the bear.

Santa was dangling by the back of his coat, in the huge dragon's claw.

"Let me go." he shouted, "Or I'll banish you to the naughty list forever."

"Ha," laughed the dragon, cruelly. "Do you think I care about your silly naughty list? I have all the presents in the world. I don't need Christmas anymore and I don't need you."

"What do you mean, you don't need me?" Santa Gulped.

"Alright," the Dragon said, sounding almost friendly now. "Let me rephrase that. I most definitely do need you."

"Oh, what a relief." said Santa, wiping his brow.

"For a little festive snack." laughed the dragon.

At that moment Lucy and the bear flew in through the roof.

"Lucky I had spare keys", said the bear, polishing his silver badge. Lucy now wore one the same, as did every elf in the room.

The cloud landed right next to the dragons toy pile, dropped of his passengers and left in quite a hurry.

"STOP." shouted Lucy

"Look Santa," smiled the dragon, "more little play mates."

"Put him down." cried the bear. "Or I'll..."

"You'll what?" snapped the dragon. "You can't do anything to me, bear. In fact I might have to eat you too."

The beast snapped up the little bear in his other claw.

"Oh no." said Lucy, "The elves looked equally lost."

"Do something, somebody." shouted one of them.

"Now what do I do?" said the frantic Lucy.

"I wonder which one I should eat first?" chortled the dragon. "What do you think, little girl?"

Lucy didn't know what to say. All seemed lost but then she saw it. On the dragons arm was the Christmas bear's green and white, Christmas pudding patterned rubber ring. That was his key to the workshop. As luck would have it there was a present at her side that was shaped like just what she needed. She picked it up and unwrapped it as fast as lightning. And then she grabbed a nail from the work bench at her side. The dragon seemed to have made up his mind about who to eat first. Both of them. He was dangling them over his wide open, pointy tooth filled mouth.

Lucy quickly loaded the nail into her Thundergirls pink princess catapult and fired.

The dragon's rubber ring exploded, with a bang. Then he cursed as he was magically sucked out through the hole in the roof. He dropped Santa and the bear safely on top of the toy pile.

"Good riddance to bad rubbish." shouted the bear, triumphantly.

"And," laughed Santa "you're definitely on the naughty list."

The dragon flew off into the night, muttering to himself, all the way.

Soon after that, he managed to particularly annoy the tooth fairy by trying to take his favourite wand. The dragon now lives on a small farm in Outer Mongolia. He is no longer a dragon, but a particularly smelly yak. Too bad really.

It turned out that the bear had a spare rubber ring in the workshop. This one magically expanded until it was a large, flying rubber dingy.

Santa quickly went to deliver the rest of his presents. Lucy and the bear flew off to collect the other chosen children. Then they had a wonderful party, with music and the best Christmas pudding and whipped cream on the planet. They danced, had reindeer rides and enjoyed the best time they'd ever had.

When the party was over, all the other children got back in the dingy. But before Lucy did, Santa stopped her.

"I don't usually do this," he winked at Lucy, "but this is a very special occasion. You have saved Christmas for the whole world."

Lucy wondered what he was going to say next.

"I am going to let you keep your key to the workshop."

"Really? " Lucy gasped." You mean I can come back?"

"Yes Lucy," smiled the bear, but you will only be able to find the workshop on Christmas eve night. And you will need this."

The bear handed her a tiny, silver whistle, on a red, silk ribbon.

"What's this for?" she asked.

"To summon a snow cloud, my dear." laughed Santa, "How else will you get here?"

"Thank you both." she said, giving them each a big hug.

As she climbed aboard her ride, she waved good bye to Santa, the elves and the reindeer. The bear dropped her off, back at her house. Then she got into bed and fell into a deep sleep, full of wonderful sweet dreams.

She awoke in the morning, with a start.

"Was it all just a dream?" she asked herself.

The window was fixed and there was no sign it had ever been broken.

But then she looked down to the foot of the bed and saw a present. It was wrapped in Christmas pudding patterned paper and the label read, 'To our hero, From the Christmas bear and associates'.

She unwrapped it to find her very own Thundergirls pink princess catapult and a little note that said 'Don't forget, the whistle is in your coat pocket. Take care now."

"What a wonderful Christmas." said Lucy, with a big grin.

Then she jumped out of bed to enjoy the rest of her magical day...

The End

Rhymes

Lee Pritchett

The Adventure of Garry the Gobble

Garry the little gobble was small and he wobbled.
And on his head was a hat with a bobble.
It was cold in his home,
By the sea, with no phone.
He couldn't order a pizza.
Or apply for a loan.
He wanted the sun to shine, hot and bright.
But it was freezing in his home, day after night.
He went to the beach, to collect some drift wood,
For a fire to warm him and to cook something good.
But the sea it did rage, and Garry got soaked.
The poor little Gobble, was really quite choked.
As he walked home, it started to snow.

A cupid came down and shot him, with a bow.
He fell in love with a boat, it was pretty and blue.
He got in the boat and found a kangaroo.
Garry and Roo, sailed to the west.
They dived under the sea, and found a pirate chest.
It was filled with doubloons, shiny and gold.
Garry and Roo were pirates now, fearless and bold.
In their mighty blue ship, they went to strange lands.
They met tribal elders and shook all their hands.
Roo showed Garry how to bounce and run.
He showed Roo how to wobble, and how to have fun.
They travelled through the lands by river and sea.
Finding wonderful things to do and be,
They met some hiding dinosaurs, and had a whale of a time.
With dinosaur music and dinosaur rhyme.
Then Garry and Roo got back in the boat.
They decided to head home, with a unanimous vote.
They sailed the seas together once more.
Then they crashed onto an island, full of fairies and wild
boar.
The fairies were the best of fun. They showed them lots of
magic.
Some of it caused big explosions, it was rather tragic.
They had more fairy fireworks and ate some fairy food.
The boars they didn't speak at all, Garry thought them rather
rude.
Then all of a sudden, there was mighty magic thunder.
Purple lightning raged on...Was coming here a blunder?
Roo picked up Garry and bounced him to the boat.
When they were back onboard, they found a little stoat.
"Take me with you?" he pleaded "I'm so scared of thunder."
"Ok," said Garry "I hope we don't go under."
They sailed and sailed, through massive waves, thousands
of feet tall.
The boat was flipped and thrown about, it wasn't good at all.
The night it fell and as they slept, they drifted through the
seas.
They woke up in the bright sun. They'd hardly scuffed their
knees.
As they looked around, they saw a familiar place,

Full of kangaroos and the entire Gobble race.

"Where've you been?" they asked at once. It was warm and sunny now.

"I've been on an adventure," said Garry "with Stoat and Roo, my bestest pals..."

The End

Spotty Backwing

Dear old Spotty Backwing, he was very slow.
His mother was a dragon, but his father.... I don't know?
She never would tell him, what happened to his daddy.
Even when he huffed and puffed, having a good paddy.
He had a big old hunch back, and a pair of wings,
And he had three tongues, good for licking things.

His wings were rather tiny, a bit small for flying.
But he wasn't bothered, so he gave up trying.
He liked his dragon tale, and thought his spots worked
And he liked his blue bow tie, he got from his friend Bert.
Bertie was a snail. He was Spotty's friend.
They'd met quite by chance, on a beach weekend.

They had both made a sand castle. Both castles looked the same.
They had a picture of that day, put into a frame.
They ate their lunch together, at twelve-o-clock each day.
They both enjoyed their salad, what more can I say?
They both were rather ponderous, and rather slow to learn.
They liked a game of chess, taking hours for each turn.
They lived in the same park, where Spotty was born,
So it was rather strange, that they hadn't met before.
One day on a picnic, Bert began a tale,
It began one summer, with a young snail.
He'd come to this park for the very first time.
And he'd met a dragon, named Nelly Divine.

They'd fallen in love, and then got married.
They'd travelled the world. Bert had been carried.
They had been to Japan and even to France,
They'd left *there* quite quickly, after only one dance.
Snails aren't quite safe in France. They're often a light snack.
Bertie swore that day he would never go back.
They flew over the clouds, but then they came home.
They missed their own park, with its sweet garden nomes.
They lived there for years, and then one day.
A baby was born and he liked to play.
Though he loved his daddy, he was just a bit tubby.
Daddy nearly got squashed, by his little bubby.
Then in the end, though the snail wasn't ready.
He had to leave, until his son grew more steady.
"So what do you think?" asked Bertie the snail.
"What?" replied spotty, scratching his tail.
"He's your father." said mum "really, he's back."
"I'm your dad." said Bertie "Now let's all have a snack."
"Daddy?" asked Spotty. He was so happy.
"Why didn't mum tell me? I love you, dear old chappy."
His parents couldn't hurt him, their dear little Spotty.
By saying he was dangerous, with his enormous botty.

But now he knew the truth, Spotty didn't mind.
They all had a bite to eat, spotty felt quite refined.
He had the best of dragon and the best of snail.
At least he wasn't slimy, leaving trails with his tail.
They were a family. Spotty was glad that he knew.
He had a flying mummy and a snail daddy too.
They were happy to be together, for ever, ever more.
So that's where he got his hunch back, and his dragon
claws...

The End

Skybear and The Moon

There was a bear with giant wings
He was best friends with a mighty king.
On the back of the bear, the king would fly,
High in the sky as the clouds blew on by.
One day on the top of a mountain up high,
They met a huge eagle, baking a pie.
The pie it was magic, and when it was ready.
It exploded and out came a thousand teddies.
The teddies had wings, they were like the Skybear.
They flew through the sky, as a flock with brown hair.
They flew over the ocean, and into the night.
They flew up to the stars and brought back moonlight.
In a jar it was kept, brilliant and bright.
Back to the king's kingdom, the bears they took flight.
The moonlight lit the palace, with a brilliant glow.
But In the night the moonlight, began to go.
In the morning they found that the moonlight was gone.
The Skybear he did cry. It had not lasted long.
So as the sun shone, he went back to the moon.

He passed a cow riding on a giant space spoon.
When he got to the moon, he found all was dark.
An old man greeted him. The man said he'd stolen the spark.
The Skybear hadn't realised what his jar had contained.
He went back down to the earth to see what remained.
At the king's palace the jar just held dust.
They needed to fix things, really they must.
"What do we do?" the king asked Skybear.
"We'll send out the teddies, to find moonlight somewhere."
Teddies went to the North Pole, teddies went to the south.
Teddies went to the desert, and the Amazon's mouth.
But there was no moonlight   for the teddies to find.
The next night it was dark, only the stars shined.
On the next day when the sun did rise,
Skybear had an idea, of where he could fly.
He took the moon jar and flew to the sun.
He scooped up some sun shine, and away he did run.
Unlike the moon's keeper, the sun's didn't mind.
The sun had such power. On it would shine.
Back to the moon, the Skybear took his jar.
He found the moon keeper in a little green car.
"Good." said the keeper "Put it in the tank."
Then go to the bonnet and turn round the crank.
As Skybear turned the handle, the moon shine returned.
The bear was so happy, a lesson he'd learned.
Don't steal from the moon's glow, then it might not shine.
If you want a nightlight, ask mummy. That's fine...

The End

The Epheline and The Fizzle Fairy

One day the Epheline went to meet Puppy
He said "Let's have a picnic, underneath a nut tree."
They went to the park, with a basket of treats.
They sat in the shade and began to eat.
Sandwiches and sticky buns, and lots of sweet tea
They were having a great time, sat under that tree.
Then over flew a sparkling, popping fairy.
She was rather pretty, but her sound was rather scary.

"Woof. Woof." said puppy "Could you please stop that sound?"
"Yes." said the Epheline "If you're staying around."
"But I'm a fizzler," said the fairy, "It's just what I do."
"I fizzle as I fly, and do magic too."
"Oh..." said the Epheline "What magic do you possess?"

"I don't know." said the fairy "Would you like to help me guess?"
"You don't know?" said the puppy "Then we'd be glad to help you see."
"Yes." smiled the Epheline "Just you two come with me."
They took the fizzling fairy, to a very special tree.
The trunk opened up, and in went the three.
Down to a basement, full of crystal balls.
In the centre was a big one. They looked inside and saw,
A thousand little fairies, flying through the air,
Sparkling fizzling and popping, to a castle's grand front stairs.
They knocked the door and then held hands, then came the surprise.
The fairies merged into one, becoming human sized.
They went inside. It was a castle full of dancing and delight.
The fairy danced around the floor, and caught a prince's sight.
The prince he fell in love with her, and she became the queen.
They had the grandest wedding the world had ever seen.
Now the prince could turn to fairies too.
"That's it." said the Epheline "There's more Fizzlers than just you."
He whistled loud and in a flash they found themselves outside.
He called a giant bird and they all went for a ride.
They flew for miles across the land, Puppy sniffed the air
Suddenly she called out. "There. There. Land down there."
"Thanks Puppy." said the Epheline. They flew down to the woods.
They followed Puppy's nose some more. At sniffing she was good.
Soon they found a little house, just right for the fairy.
"Oh," said Puppy and Epheline. "It's too small for you and me."
So the Epheline shrunk himself and Puppy, with a toot of magic whistle.
In they went and found some fairies, and lots of bright pink thistles.

"Hello." said the Fizzle fairy "What are these thistles for?"
"Oh, we're glad you're here," said the other fairies, "without you life's a bore."
"We've never met, have we?" the first fairy asked them.
"You're our sister." said the others. "Please don't leave again."
"The thistles, they are magic." They keep us safe from harm.
"How lovely." said the Epheline "They have a certain charm."
Puppy pricked her paw on one and she began to fly.
Up she went to the little ceiling. She began to cry.
"I don't like flying on my own." she told the Epheline.
So he jumped and got her, then healed her paw, with a magic rhyme.
"Fulifa Fillifa Fulafalloo.
 You're my best friend and I'll always help you.
Hold out your poor paw and I'll make it alright.
And we'll have hot chocolate and marsh mallows tonight."
The fairies went and found true love. They lived happily ever after.
Puppy went to the Epheline's for tea and they shared in lots of laughter.
They'd helped the fairies find each other, but what else had they done?
They'd had such a jolly, lovely day, filled with lots of fun...

The End

Lee Pritchett

Princess Purdy's Birthday Cake

On princess Purdy's birthday, she made a special wish.
She wished for cake and ice-cream, served up in a dish.
She asked the fairytale baker, to bake a special treat,
With icing and with chocolate. It would taste so sweet.
It had to be quite magical, with a power like no other.
Maybe it could bring her a new sister, or a brother.
She had a jolly party, with all her bestest friends.
They played pass the parcel and pin the tail. She wished it
would never end.

She wore her bestest dress. It was colourful and shiny.
She had the palace decorated, even the outside trees

The party had such music as to make anyone happy.
But Purdy wished for something more, a new special puppy chappy.
Then the baker arrived, with her special cake.
Purdy blew the candle, wishing her day it would make.
A sparkling breeze filled the palace, with a giggling and a bark.
Two small puppies appeared. They were happy as a lark.
The little girl pup was called Lucy. She was like a ball of fluff.
The boy pup was called Charlie. He was hansom. He was tough.

"I'm your new brother." said Charlie. "Lucy's your sister too."
"We'll be family forever. And we'll always love you."
They each brought her a present, one silver bone, one gold.
Charlie showed her how to bark a song to make you bold.
Purdy felt so brave now, that she went out to the courtyard.
She chased an owl. They laughed and laughed. They'd never laughed so hard.
Purdy was so happy. The king and queen were too.
This was such a brilliant day. They couldn't believe it was true.

They ate some cake with ice-cream. It was tasty as can be.
Then they had some lemonade and a cup of tea.
They danced and sang, then played more games. The day was full of magic,
More special than any day before. The opposite to tragic.
The puppies and their parents, were happy ever more.
Especially princess Purdy, She was the most joyful of all...

The End

Lee Pritchett

Eddie and The Biscuit Mines

Eddie the Labrador woke one day, hungry for a snack
He went downstairs, to the kitchen and filled up his back
pack.
He headed to the garden, to eat his tasty treats.
He had some cheese and biscuits, and some tasty meats.
As he ate a sausage, the ground beneath him sunk.
He fell for miles and miles, and landed with a *plunk*.
His breakfast was high above and he was down below
But his tummy was still rumbling, but for food, where could
he go?
Deep down in the earth, how could he find a nibble?

He didn't want to chew on worms, or eat gravel bits for kibble.

Eddie was in a tunnel, so he took a walk.

He wished he could find custard creams, or maybe some roast pork.

He sniffed the air and thought he picked up something rather nice.

It smelt like chicken and noodles, with a little rice.

He followed the smell. It led him to an even bigger tunnel,
Where little men mined biscuits, and poured them down a funnel.

"Where do they go?" asked Eddie, nibbling on a treat.

It tasted like a six course meal, with noodles and roast beef.

"To the biscuit king." said the men "why don't you go and see?"

So Eddie jumped on down the shoot and he shouted "Weeeeeeee."

He slid down with the biscuits and landed in a pile,
Of food, quite like a mountain. He slid down that with style.

When he reached the bottom, he found a big fat cat.

He was munching on the biscuits, with a gold crown for a hat.

"Are you the biscuit king?" asked Eddie. The pussy he said "yes."

"They are my mummy's recipe. She's really quite the chef."

They ate biscuits together, till Eddie was plump too.

He jumped into a catapult and back on home he flew.

He landed in own bed, slim again once more.

He licked his lips and sat up and he gave a yawn...

The End

Sydney The Super Hedgehog

Sydney the super hedgehog was a super chap.
He liked to fly through space, and he wore a super cap.
He lived on a farm, and liked to save the day.
He rescued little children, and put out fires in hay.
He had super hedgehog strength and super hedgehog speed.
Every race he went in, he was always in the lead.
Once he raced a cheetah, and little Sydney won.
The cheetah sulked off home. He didn't think it fun.
Another day he raced a dog, and boy that dog could race.
He was faster than the cheetah, and had a very furry face.
Sydney could hardly keep up. He ran with all his might.
He even tried flying. Something wasn't right.
They raced around the farm. They raced around the wood.
They raced through fields of barley. Boy this dog was good.
His name was Rocket Charlie, the super running hound.
Faster than any hedgehog. He learned racing at the pound.

When he'd found an owner, he still wanted someone to race.
He'd heard of super Sydney, and he thought that he'd be ace.
"Ok. You win." said Sydney "That was a worthy race."
"Now we've sped across the land, let's try in outer space."
"Rowwwww!" said Charlie. "I don't think so."
"That's not a place for me to go?"
"We all do have our talents. I'm land. You're outer space."
"Ok," smiled Sydney, "that was a brilliant race..."

The End

Pudding land

There once was a place full of magical plants.
Where the flowers were made of cake, and the ants they could dance.
The tree's dripped with treacle. They were made out of sponge.
The birds they liked to sword fight, to leap and to lunge.
The grass was made of chocolate. It melted under foot.
But when you dipped marshmallows in it, boy it was good.
One day there was a party, and all were invited.
The birds, they were ecstatic. The ants they were excited.
But someone else arrived. He was tall and he was fluffy.
He was big. He was purple. With him was a puppy.
The Epheline said hello, and ate a lot of cake.
Puppy lapped up lots of chocolate from the ants' chocolate lake.

The ants were not happy. Neither were the birds.
They asked them both to leave, and said some nasty words.
"This is our food." they said, all together.
"But we just want to be friends." said Puppy, "like birds of a feather."
This won some of the birds round, but the others raised their swords.
The ants, they yelled attack and pulled on a chord.
A giant net fell on the Epheline, so Puppy barked out loud.
The net disappeared by magic. The Epheline was so proud.
Puppy was learning magic and getting quite good.
The Epheline whistled and made even more pud.
Cream cakes and buns, Swiss rolls and other treats.
The ants and birds were so happy. They so loved their sweets.
They got back to their party. They ate and drank tea.
Who knew some new friends, could make you so happy.
They all danced together and played games galore.
They sword fought with sticks, and had marshmallow wars.
They sung lots of songs, and had such fun.
They swam in the chocolate lake, and then went for a run.
It was a close race, but puppy was the winner.
Then they sat down and ate a chocolate dinner.
"What a terrific day." Puppy said, with a bark.
They continued celebrating, until it was dark...

The End

The Bear With the Magical Stone

Once there was a polar bear. He was rather chubby.
He had a very special stone, he called it Pebble Cubby.

When he rubbed the stone, the bear got special powers.
He could do kung-foo, and talk to all the flowers.
The kung-foo polar bear was a hero to the plants.
When they saw him flip and kick they liked to sing and dance.
One day the kung-foo bear, met a nasty seal.
It called him Mr Chubby Chub, and the bear gave a squeal.
He rubbed on Pebble Cubby, but something went wrong.
His powers did come, but the flowers gave a song.
"Don't fight this silly seal, my friend."
"Fights don't help a thing."
"Simply make a wish."
"And see what it might bring."
So the bear he made a wish. He wished for a better way.
There was a brilliant flash. And he landed in some hay.

He'd fallen from the sky and landed in a wood,
At the mouth of a cave, where two people stood.
One wore stripy pyjamas, another was a bear.
He had a magical jewel and very furry hair.
This other bear had made a wish. He'd wished for a new friend.
The Pyjama man was Mr Squiggle. Some time together they'd spend.
They were now the three best friends, there could ever be.
With magic they could have some fun, make a wish or three.
The polar bear was upset though, that his stone was just a stone.
But he tapped it on a rock, and what came to be shown?

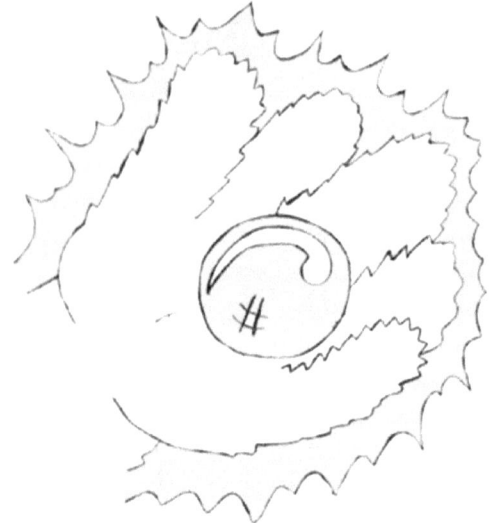

Inside was purest gold, for wishes full of fun.
But he still loved to practice kung-foo, just for showing everyone.
The flowers sung once more for him. They sang of friendship true.
A magic bear and a squiggle man, what's a kung-foo bear to do?

The End

www.ingramcontent.com/pod-product-compliance
Lightning Source LLC
Chambersburg PA
CBHW030344030726
47499CB00003B/895